TAKING CHANCES

A HOPE HERRING COZY MYSTERY
BOOK 13

J. A. WHITING
NELL MCCARTHY

Copyright 2023 J.A. Whiting and Whitemark Publishing

Cover copyright 2023 Signifer Book Design

Formatting by Signifer Book Design

Proofreading by Donna Rich (donnarich@me.com) and Riann Kohrs (riannkohrs.com)

This book is a work of fiction. Names, characters, places, or incidents are products of the author's imagination or are used fictitiously. Any resemblance to locales, actual events, or persons, living or dead, is entirely coincidental.

All rights reserved.

No part of this publication can be reproduced or transmitted in any form or by any means, electronic or mechanical, without permission in writing from J. A. Whiting.

To hear about new books and book sales, please sign up for my mailing list at:
jawhiting.com

❦ Created with Vellum

With thanks to our readers

Dream big

1

Hope sat at the back of the auditorium, along with most of the other teachers. A few stood against the walls, more interested in the students in their seats than the students on the stage. Hope had an interest in both as her daughter was getting ready for her solo. While she had heard Cori sing the song a hundred times at home, the true test would come when Cori stood on stage and belted out "On A Clear Day." Hope knew Cori could do it. The question was stage fright. Could Cori stand up to the wilting stares of her classmates?

Hope remembered her own battles with the jitters that always arose when performing in the annual school play or show. She had volunteered and auditioned all through elementary school and high school, and she always obtained a role. She was never the lead; her voice simply wasn't as good as Veronica Pierce's, yet Hope nailed significant parts for which she was forever grateful. Performing had taught her she could overcome the "jitters."

Her stage career ended in college when she realized she was never going to out-sing the music majors whose voices had been carefully coached for a decade. Hope came to terms with her failed dream although she had never really subscribed to the belief that she was destined for the stage, movies, or recording contracts. In a way, teaching had become her stage, and she was good at it. That seemed more than enough.

The small band sat in front of the brightly lit stage and while not large in numbers, they produced a quality sound. Brad Edie, the music teacher and band director, managed the students and taught them well. Still young, his good looks certainly helped persuade the fledgling musicians to do their best. Hope believed he hadn't served long enough to become jaded. She knew more than one teacher whose attitude had turned black, men and women who had checked out, simply waiting for retirement to send them off to Florida. She couldn't fathom that sort of career.

Not yet, anyway.

The lights dimmed.

A spot flashed to the corner of the stage.

Cori smiled, started across the stage, and launched into the song. Hope smiled at her in return, listening and basking in the success that was her daughter. In Hope's world, parents were still allowed to share the limelight their children achieved, but she would never take any bows. It was Cori's night. It was all about a teenager spreading her wings. Hope experienced a joy she hadn't often felt since the death of her husband. She knew he would have been more than a little proud. He would have joined the other fathers in the center aisle, men with video cameras who recorded every note. Doug would have had a library of videos, things he might watch as he aged. But he wouldn't age. After several years, Hope had come to terms with his death.

Suddenly, she noticed a change in the crowd. Where the students had been a bit restless with some of the other performers, they sat in rapt attention to Cori's singing. Hope had to admit that Cori did sound professional. That was something. She didn't sound that good in her own bedroom. Hope guessed that the sound system and acoustics made the difference.

Adele Wells leaned close to Hope. Adele was the neighbor down the street and a good friend to Hope, and her daughter Lottie was Cori's best friend.

"She's fantastic," Adele whispered.

"Thanks," Hope answered, chills running down her back. She was so happy for her daughter.

She knew the accolades would mostly come after the show, but she was glad to hear it from Adele. Lottie was in the show, too, but she was a dancer and didn't have a solo. That was how it was. Talent was never evenly distributed among people. Those who believed that every student arrived with the same capacity to perform were the people who had never taught school.

Cori finished with a flourish, and the crowd clapped and stood in an ovation Hope wasn't sure Cori's performance merited. Still, she stood with the rest, more than thrilled for her daughter. The fact Cori was pretty and slender only added to the enjoyment of her voice.

"She's got it," Adele said as they clapped. "You need to find a voice coach."

"No, Cori needs to find a voice coach," Hope said.

"You're not going to help her?"

"I'll definitely help her, but the desire and effort have to come from her."

"You sound like you don't want her to succeed."

"I've always tried not to be a helicopter mom. I'm not here to tell her what she should want. Don't get me wrong, I will certainly step in if I think she's headed in the wrong direction, but her ambitions have to be hers. I've seen too many parents living their dreams through their children."

"I suppose you're right, and frankly, I don't envy you. In a way, I'm glad Lottie doesn't have that kind of talent. I would probably be the worst stage mom in existence."

Hope laughed. "I hear you. Promise me that if you see me on some TV talent show, you'll send me a text and tell me how dumb I look."

"You laugh now, but it won't be so funny when the showrunners and producers start showing up at your door. The world is begging for talent, and your daughter has it."

"She does, but talent isn't enough. I doubt she's hungry enough to battle the sharks that are out there."

Cori left the stage, and the audience settled. Hope sat, and the stage filled with another act, a scene from *Romeo and Juliet*. There was something about Shakespeare's play that spoke to teenagers. They fell for the romance, forgetting that the play ended badly. They believed the saying, "Love conquers all." Love wasn't enough. It was never enough. Romeo and Juliet paid a price for falling for each other. It was that simple and that tragic.

After the show, Hope waited in the vestibule for her daughter, where several parents and teachers approached and congratulated Hope on her daughter's performance. She disregarded the praise. She hadn't done anything. Cori was the one who had earned the accolades. Still, Hope did feel a good bit of pride. She had done something right. That much was obvious.

"Cori was fantastic."

Hope turned to the voice she recognized. "She was, wasn't she? I'm very happy for her. I'm glad you enjoyed the performance, Virginia."

Virginia Zalar taught math and was a year younger than Hope. Virginia was a North Carolina native and a graduate of NC State University. Pretty, with long blond hair and brown eyes, she was a regular jogger. Hope had been invited to run with Virginia more than once, and she had always meant to take up the sport, but there simply wasn't enough time.

"Thank you," Hope said.

"She makes all of us wish we could sing."

"I sang a bit when I was in school. I wasn't that good. Cori commands all the talent in the family."

"Don't be modest, Hope. You might not be the best singer, but you are our resident Sherlock Holmes. Everyone knows that." Virginia smiled.

The young woman wore black stretch pants that were all the rage. A longish red top accentuated her figure. To Hope, Virginia was just what a woman should be ... no fat, lots of energy, and a first-class mind. Hope knew more than one teacher who wished they looked as good and were as smart as Virginia.

"My reputation is kind of overblown. I got lucky on a couple of cases," Hope demurred. "Truthfully, it was the police who did all the heavy lifting."

"Not from what I hear. You not only solve the cases, you take on some risk. I don't think I could ever do that."

"Need instills courage sometimes ... but more often, foolishness."

They laughed together, even as Brad Edie worked his way through the throng.

This show was Brad's brainchild as he'd recruited the on-stage talent, as well as the backstage help. He had once told Hope that it was just as difficult to find good people to work the curtains and lights as it was to recruit singers and dancers. Most people didn't realize how much manpower a production needed.

"Hope." Brad beamed. "You should be very proud. Cori was the hit of the night."

"Thanks to you," Hope replied. "The music and production were flawless."

Brad laughed. He wore a pink bow tie with his starched, blue, small-print shirt. His pants were pressed and creased, as always. The young man always dressed well. Hope guessed he spent most of his teacher's salary on outfits and shoes, but since he was single, he could afford to splurge a little. Although no one knew for certain, it was thought that he was gay. That might have bothered some people in a different decade, but it was just another characteristic to Hope.

"You have no idea what it's like backstage," Brad said. "Something is always, and I do mean always, going wrong. Panic is a well-known aspect of the theater."

Brad flashed his dark, blue eyes at Virginia. The blue eyes accompanied coal-black hair and a lean face. Brad was more than a little handsome. Half the girls in his classes had secret crushes on him. Hope could see why.

"How did you like the show, Virginia?" Brad asked.

"You get better every year," Virginia answered. "I was just congratulating Hope on Cori's performance."

"She was fantastic, wasn't she?" Brad asked. "I think I've found my lead for the spring musical. And, yes, we're doing a musical this year. I just need to find a young man who can keep up with Cori."

"That shouldn't be difficult," Hope said. "I noticed more than one good voice in the glee club."

"Yes, we are blessed with some talent. Of course, they have to be able to listen well also. That is maybe the hardest skill students need to learn ... as we all know."

Brad looked from woman to woman, and Hope knew they all agreed. Most students weren't renowned for their listening skills.

"Oops," Virginia said, "I see Walt waiting by the door. Time for me to run. Brad, great job. Hope, I expect to hear wonderful things from Cori."

"That she got an A on a math quiz?" Hope kidded. "Now, that would be great news."

Virginia laughed and shook her head. "She's doing fine. I wish all my students were doing as well."

Hope watched Virginia hurry for the door. More than one man watched along with Hope.

"May I ask you a question?" Brad asked.

"Certainly," Hope answered. "Fire away."

"Have you thought about voice lessons for Cori?"

"You know, you're the second person who asked me that question tonight. I'll give you the short answer. No, I haven't considered lessons."

"You might think on it. I know I'm just a public school music teacher, but I have spent a few summers at various resort theaters. I think I'm a fair judge of talent."

"How many of those talented singers ended up with any sort of career?"

"A couple, and that would be about average. I won't sugarcoat the work involved. For every person who makes it, a hundred go by the wayside. It's an industry that takes talent and berates it until there is a diamond-hard glaze or the person gives up. It's a computer problem writ large."

"Computer problem?"

"There was a time when I thought I might like to pursue a career in software engineering. I had an advisor who knew more than a thing or two about the intelligence and grit needed. There was a lot of math involved and a mammoth amount of logic. I won't bore you with the details, but he told me I was not equipped to handle the advanced requirements. I argued, of course, and he told me of a problem in the science. He said that there was no way to determine when a computer program should be stopped. We all know of apps that suddenly go off the grid and run for days on end. Most of us decide that our computer needs to be stopped and rebooted, but, we can't know if the computer would generate an answer in the next second. We wait ... and wait ... and wait. Stop? Who knows?"

"You're saying this applies to actors and singers?"

"Precisely. I've seen actors, very good actors, plow through gig after gig, convinced that the next gig will propel them into the limelight. The stars will align, and there will be an agent or producer in the second row, someone who will notice their brilliance and change the actor's life forever. It rarely, rarely happens that way. So, the actor doesn't know when to quit; when to shut down the process and reboot. One more gig, and maybe he or she will make it."

"Wait, didn't you just tell me to start Cori with singing lessons?"

He laughed. "I did. That's the upside. I had to give you the downside also. There is no guarantee. I know she'll get gigs. With practice, she might do very well. Will she know when to quit? No one can tell her that."

"I think I'll let her make that decision. Do you know of any voice coaches ... in case she asks?"

"I'm one." He chuckled. "Not just piano. I teach voice, too."

"Great. I won't have to import you from Raleigh or someplace."

"Not yet. She may well eclipse my limited help. Then, you'll have other choices."

Hope smiled. "Don't get ahead of this, Brad. It's one night in a school talent show."

He grinned. "We all dream, Hope. Every one of us. Now, I have to placate a number of other parents. Ta-ta."

Hope watched Brad wade through the crowd. Before she could consider his advice, someone tugged her sleeve.

"Ready to go?" Cori asked.

Hope hugged her daughter. "Congratulations. You were wonderful tonight."

"I'm exhausted. I never dreamed this would be so ... draining."

"Performing requires energy, lots of energy." Hope wrapped an arm around Cori's shoulders. "Be glad it's Friday. No school tomorrow."

In the car, Cori stared out the window. "Was I good? Really?"

"You were very good," Hope answered. "Everyone sure thought so."

"I was afraid of that. I guess I need a job."

2

"You're too young to get a job," Hope said.

"Not a real job, just something that will pay a few bucks."

"Babysitting," Hope suggested.

"I don't want to babysit. That's not a real job. It's not steady enough."

"Why do you need a steady income?"

"I don't need a steady income. I need a piano, and I don't think you have the money for that so I want to earn the money."

"I see," Hope said. "Why a piano?"

"So I can learn to play and accompany myself when I sing. I think lots of very good composers learned music on a piano."

"You want to study music, create songs, and sing them?"

"That would seem to be a way forward. Look, Mom, I really, really like to sing. I'm good at it. I think I might be able to become even better. I know you'll caution me. I know there are a million girls just like me, girls with good voices who dream about singing as a career. I also know that some of those girls are going to make it, but not through luck. They'll ... I'll have to really work at it."

"I see. Well, you're correct. I can't afford a piano right now. I think I can swing some lessons though."

"What good are lessons if I don't have a piano? I mean, I need to practice."

"You can learn a lot, even if you don't have a piano. Of course, much of that learning can be done online. I'm certain there are a number of sites that address music theory and composition."

"Again, that's all good, but it's not hands-on. Every good singer has to be able to practice for real."

"And perform. You'll need to perform also. Can you do that online?"

"Yeah, I mean, there are apps that will allow me to post what I record. If I'm good enough, I'll get some followers, but I still need something to produce the music."

"Let me think about it."

"Please, Mom, really think about it. I've never really felt like this about anything before. I don't know if that's good or bad, but it's new, you know?"

"Cori, if you dedicate yourself to this pursuit, I'll join you. I'll do all I can to help make your dream come true."

Cori smiled. "Thanks. I ... I think I have a chance. I don't want it to pass me by."

When they arrived at home, their cat Bijou greeted them at the door, and Cori and Hope patted the feline and gave her some cheek scratches.

Max was waiting in the kitchen, and he smiled when Hope entered. Max was a century-old ghost, who had come with the house when she bought it. He had hung around in order to solve his own murder. Although that had been accomplished, with Hope's help, Max had not moved on. He had stayed with the house, which she appreciated. That night, he wore a black tuxedo, complete with black studs and cummerbund.

"I am ready to applaud Cori," Max said. "I take it her debut was memorable, and I mean that in a good way."

"It certainly was," Hope said. "She was the hit of

the show, and I think she discovered that she likes the applause."

"Ah, yes, I believe we all love accolades. I never plied myself across the stage. My talents lay elsewhere. I did, however, meet performers. They were mostly a sorry lot. They worked hard for not much money. They thrived on the joy of their performance and the response from the audience. I suppose that can be a kind of aphrodisiac."

"It can certainly be addicting. We all know of people who lived for the show and were the worse for it."

Cori walked in, and Max clapped loudly.

"Bravo," Max said. "I have been informed that you were the hit of the evening. I knew that would happen."

"Thank you, Max," Cori said. "I'm sorry you didn't have the opportunity to be there, but I appreciate your support."

"It's the least I can do. Your mother seems to think you've been bitten by the fame bug. You like the footlights?"

"I'm afraid I do, but I love singing even more than the attention. I know I shouldn't dream, but it was such a rush."

"Now, she wants lessons," Hope said, "and a piano."

"Completely understandable," Max said. "I wish I were in a position to acquire a grand piano for you. I am not, so I can only sit on the sidelines and encourage you."

"You can find me a job," Cori said. "I'll buy the piano if I can work somewhere."

"Ah, yes, that makes sense. Well, I'm certain the Internet lists any number of jobs. We'll find one for you, as I have all the time in the world to search."

"Thank you. Could you make it an interesting job that pays a lot of money?"

Max laughed. "In all the years I've been here, the wishes have not changed. Everyone wants a job that will inspire them and one that comes with an inordinate salary. I'm afraid those jobs are rare, Cori."

"But, you have all day, Max. You'll find one for me." Cori grinned.

"I believe child labor laws have changed since I was a boy," Max said. "The days of sending a young girl to be a maid in a rich home are gone."

"I'll leave it to you," Cori told him. "Good night. Come on, Bijou." The cat happily followed Cori to her bedroom.

"Good night, and dream pleasant dreams," Max said.

"I'll stop by on my way to bed," Hope said.

Cori disappeared, leaving Hope and Max in the kitchen.

"You do know that she faces a difficult, uphill climb," Max said.

"I do know, and I am not convinced she'll make it. Perseverance was never one of her strong points."

"You may be surprised this time. Some people find their niche early in life. If they do, they adopt a single vision. When I was young, my best friend decided he would become a ship's captain. In those days, you didn't go to school to learn to captain. You signed onto a ship and worked like the devil. If you showed aptitude and desire, the captain might take you under his wing and teach you about navigation, charts, and weather. Many a ship was lost because the captain didn't recognize the makings of a typhoon. There were no satellites or weather stations in those days. Anyway, Todd signed onto a whaler named *The Calypso*. Whalers were tough berths, as they would spend a year or more away from port. When the ship returned, I went to the docks to greet my friend. He wasn't there. I learned that the ship had stopped in Macao, after a run-in with a bad storm. Todd had jumped ship. I was told there was a woman involved, but that was the usual explanation. I don't know. Over the years, there were rumors that Todd had acquired his own ship. He became the captain of a steamer that plied the routes from Pacific island to Pacific island. I don't know the truth of that. I like to think he had achieved his goal. I like to think that we all do, in one form or another."

"I don't know if that's possible," Hope said. "So many people develop impossible or nearly impossible wishes. I mean, you can't expect a small, slow man to play professional basketball."

"I agree. We all face limitations."

"My father used to call it the wall. We all reach a time and place where we hit the wall. For one reason or another, we're stuck there. We can't continue to improve, despite our best efforts. I would argue with him about it. I thought my talents had no limits. I wasn't as wise as he was."

"The wall. That is an apt metaphor, Mrs. Herring. There are walls out there. Some we can scale, some we can't. I suspect running into the wall can be a bitter pill for some people."

"Acceptance is the key, Max. Once you've come to terms with your limits, you can be happy again."

"Words of wisdom, words of wisdom. I am heading to the office and the computer, Mrs. Herring. Perhaps, I can happen upon an affordable piano."

"That would be a godsend. Have a good night."

Max disappeared, and Hope decided it was time for bed. The nagging voice inside her head said that Cori would be just fine—even if she didn't get a piano. It really wasn't the piano that Hope was worried about. The world was filled with stories about celebrities who followed the path of drugs and alcohol. Fame was fleeting, as all Roman emperors were reminded. It wasn't what happened when fame arrived. It was what happened when fickle fame left. Not many people possessed the courage and strength to bid fame adieu.

Hope was still pondering the problem the next morning as she brewed her first cup of coffee. She felt like a gambler who studied her cards and tried to fashion a good bet. The cards were too good to toss away, and yet, they were far from comprising the best hand possible. What were the odds? What sort of bet should be made now? She knew how to play the game. Place a bet, and wait while the others made their bets. Read their faces and their minds. Who had a better hand? Who had a worse one? The hardest part was not the bet. It was the next one. Starting down the path required resources. Was her hand good enough? When would enough be enough?

"Good morning," Cori said as she went about pouring her morning cereal.

"Good morning," Hope answered. "Max went online last night, trying to find you an affordable piano."

"Great. I can't wait. Oh, yes, I can. He has to find me a job first. Even an affordable piano is unaffordable right now."

"That got me thinking. What do you say about a keyboard?"

"Keyboard?"

"Yep, a full-size keyboard that you can practice on. It's not all wire and hammers, but it would produce the proper sound. It would require practice and instruction."

"Pedals?"

"I don't know. I'd have to do some research, but I have to believe that a keyboard would be cheaper than a piano. Then, after your first album goes platinum, you can afford the piano of your dreams."

Cori squinted for a moment as if thinking.

"You're trying to start with a minimal investment, aren't you?"

"I expect to be repaid from whatever job you manage to land."

"That means it's also my minimum investment, I think."

"That's just the hardware investment. There are the lessons, which will cost much more than the piano over time."

"I think I can learn to play the piano quickly."

"I agree. You're young, and you have good motor skills, but the lessons are never-ending. What you learn this week dovetails into next week, and that week feeds the week after. It's like buying a house."

"Buying a house? Is this another teachable moment?"

"It is, and you know you love them."

Cori rolled her eyes and spooned cereal into her mouth.

"Acquiring a house is easy," Hope said.

Cori grunted at that.

"The real problem is maintenance. As soon as a house is finished, it starts to deteriorate. Appliances wear out. Paint fades. Carpets and rugs fray. Faucets leak. Light bulbs fail. There are a thousand things that can and do go wrong. Many of these problems can be avoided with careful maintenance. Clean the appliances. Repaint on schedule. Cut the grass and prune the trees. Most people, though, don't think that way. When they price a house, they think of acquisition, what will it cost in down payment money and mortgage payments. If monthly bills and mortgage eat up all available earnings, the house will soon be overcome by time. That little repair that should have been made when it was discovered, grew into a much larger repair that requires dipping into savings or borrowing more money. Borrowing should be avoided unless the money will add to the value of the house. Regular upkeep should come from earnings. Remember that. In almost all instances, people don't prepare for lifetime costs. They think of acquisition only. It's like buying a new, huge TV and then not having enough income to pay for the cable hookup."

"I understand," Cori mumbled.

"Good. Because your piano lessons will not come cheap. How do you feel about Mr. Edie?"

Cori smiled. "He's a good teacher."

3

Hope found Brad Edie in his band room, a smallish space filled with music stands, raised dais, some recording equipment, a conductor's podium, and various instrument cases pushed against the walls. He was busy with his phone, holding up one finger to her as he finished his call.

"Don't tell me," he said to Hope. "I'm late for bus duty?"

"No, no, you don't have duty until next week ... I think. You better check your schedule."

"Believe me, I will, as I've been informed by the assistant principal that if I miss one more morning, I'll be docked. I can't afford to be docked. By the way, when did the school adopt docking as a punishment?"

"When adding an extra week of bus duty didn't work," Hope kidded.

"That would work for me. I hate bus duty. What can I do for you?"

"First, I want to congratulate you on a very successful talent show. I've heard nothing but praise."

"The show is only as good as the talent. It's like karaoke night at the local pub. Good voices breed success, but screeching probably sells more drinks. You have to have a way to combat the awful sounds."

Hope chuckled. "Sounds like you've done some research in that area."

"It's great fun, really. People have their favorite songs that they think they can perform. Most do a passable job. All get better as the night wears on."

"Better looking, too."

He laughed. "Indeed. So...."

"Yes, so. So, last night Cori caught the bug. She saw the stars in the sky and thought she could join them. I'm fine with that. Everyone should have a dream."

"What's yours?" Brad asked her.

"A condo on the beach."

"In that respect, we think alike." Brad wore a pink, green, and yellow bow tie, along with a chambray shirt and jeans. He looked like a model straight out of GQ.

"Anyway, there is no way Cori will reach her goal without help. Her voice needs training. Her onstage presence needs tweaking. I'm sure there are any number of areas that she could improve."

"Indeed, the Internet is filled with people and companies that promise the moon—for a price. And there are any number of girls just like Cori, who think a few hundred dollars will get them an agent and a gig at the Grand Ole Opry."

"Doesn't work that way?" Hope smiled, knowing full well it didn't.

"Most of the so-called agents out there are bogus. Oh, they might have a license of some sort and maybe an office, but they don't have access to the producers and directors who can hire and fire. They talk big and drop names, but they're generally parasites feeding on youthful fantasies."

"How does someone break in then?"

"No one breaks in without the goods. You have to have a voice, which is the most important asset. You have to develop a stage presence, so people will want to hear you in person. You have to be attractive. Well, you don't have to be a knockout, but it certainly helps. The better you look with your tummy bared, the more people will watch. Your job is to sell recordings and put people in concert seats. Sounds easy. It's not."

"How long can it take to get work?"

He shook his head. "If you really want good advice, I'd tell you to knock that bug out of her head right now. Sunday church is filled with people who have great voices and are happy. The alleys and streets of tinsel town are littered with those who pursued the wrong dream."

"It's all about regret, isn't it?"

"Regret?"

"The amount of risk one is willing to take is proportional to the amount of regret one will feel later. For Cori, I have to ask myself if she will feel worse for trying and failing than she would by not trying at all. Will she regret not maximizing her voice every day of her adult life? Or will she look back and be glad she'd made the effort?"

"You make a strong argument, Hope. Do you want me to put out some feelers? Do you want an agent for her? A vocalist summer camp? What?"

"Well, for starters, I want your honest opinion. Does Cori have any chance of making a career of her singing?"

He stroked his chin, as if unsure about what he had to say.

"I think she has a good voice that might become a remarkable voice through practice and dedication. So, I would recommend two ways forward. One, she needs a voice coach. She needs to work on range and pitch. She has a good ear, and that helps. Lessons and drills will make her better. Two, I would tell you to get her gigs and opportunities for performance. A lot of famous singers got their start in church. Religious rituals often involve a lot of singing and chances to solo. There are weddings, parties, birthdays, and any number of special occasions. You might try karaoke, but I don't recommend that. Too many drunks and critics. Oh, you can look for a band, something local and small that might work on weekends. She might earn enough to pay for her lessons."

"Bottom line?"

"Bottom line is the road is filled with potholes, traps, and the bleached bones of the million girls who went before. Yep, the palace at the end of the road is spectacular, but very, very few reach it."

"So, don't let her start?"

"Regret? Isn't that the final thumb on the scales?"

Hope nodded. "Indeed, it is."

Brad looked past Hope and waved. "Virginia, come in. What can I do for you?"

Hope turned to find the blonde hurrying forward, a little smile on her face.

"Brad, I have a favor to ask," Virginia said. "I saw that you don't have bus duty this week. Could you possibly sub for me tomorrow? I have a parent coming in before classes start. You know, people who need to get to work like to meet early."

"Not a problem," he said. "Tell you what, since I have a very sketchy memory, send me a text to remind me. Otherwise, we'll both skip."

"You're a lifesaver. Remind me to bring you some donuts."

"Consider yourself reminded."

With a wave, Virginia hurried out.

"Donuts?" Hope asked. "You're too easy. You should have charged her a week of bus duty."

Brad laughed. "I didn't think of that. Next time, I'll negotiate better. You better get going."

"Yep, just one more thing. Would you be willing to coach Cori? I don't know what you charge, but I think you have a good rapport with her."

"I'll be happy to coach her. Tell you what, let me look at my schedule. I'll pick a day and time. I'll send that in an email, along with my rate. That work?"

"Perfect. I'm sure Cori will be on board." Hope moved toward the door. "Whatever you do, tell her the truth. Don't make it worse than it is, or better. She has to know what the road ahead looks like."

"I'll do my best. I'll encourage when it's needed and give criticism when that's needed. It won't be sugar and spice."

"All the better."

Hope hurried out and headed for her classroom. As she passed Virginia's room, she noticed that the young woman was at her desk, busy with something. Hope couldn't help but wonder why she wasn't outside with the arriving buses. Then, the truth struck Hope. Virginia had roped some other teacher into doing bus duty that morning. Hope shook her head. Virginia had a whole circle of teachers who subbed for her, one day at a time. It was easy to get a teacher for a day. A week was a different story.

Hope gave Cori the news on the ride home from school.

"Whew, thanks," Cori said. "I did an online search for voice lessons and got like twenty-four million hits."

"It takes more than an hour or two to wade through that."

"Don't I know it. And, I'll pay you back, I promise. Just as soon as I get a job."

"I'll let Mr. Edie talk to you about jobs and prospects. You can repay me with diligence. Do the practice he expects of you. Do it with purpose. There are a lot of people who practice something, and while they do it every day, they never make sure that their technique is flawless. If you do it wrong, you're building a bad habit. Make sense?"

"Perfect practice makes perfect?"

"It does little good to ingrain the wrong thing."

"I'll remember that. When's my first lesson?"

"He's sending me an email with a schedule. It'll be soon."

When they arrived home, Hope reminded her daughter, "Finish your homework before doing anything else."

Max was not in the kitchen when mother and daughter entered, but the cat trotted into the room to give the women a happy greeting.

"Where's Max?" Cori asked. "I want to give him the good news."

"Try my office," Hope said. "He's probably searching the net, looking for a job for you."

"I hope he found one. I know you said not to worry about that, but I have to pay my own way."

"Why is that?"

"Lottie."

"Lottie?"

"Lottie never pays her own way. Her parents give her money, and they pay for everything she does."

"So? What's wrong with that?"

"She's never thankful, Mom. She gets something new, and she acts like she deserves it. She always wants something new, always. She has to have it, and if she doesn't get it, she's mad. Worse, she never finishes anything."

"What do you mean?"

"When she was seven, she wanted to be a ballerina. She liked wearing the tights. Did she take it seriously? No. She went to a few lessons, didn't really try very hard, and quit. The slippers hurt her toes. That's what she told her mother. When she was nine, she went out for soccer. She liked the uniforms. Her mother took her to practice, but Lottie never practiced very hard. She played because the coach had to put everyone in the game. Did she finish the season? Nope. In school, she tried out for cheerleader. She was cut after the first session. Not even her money could put her on the squad. She joined the computer club but never went. I can't think of a single thing she's ever finished. There's always something wrong with the coach or the practices or whatever. She never finishes. She doesn't have to. It's not her money."

Hope was stunned. She had no idea her daughter knew so much about her best friend. More important, Cori had managed to learn something from Lottie's behavior.

"So, you think spending her mom's money is the reason she doesn't finish things?"

"Yeah. There's a girl in our class named Maria. She went with us for a pizza night. She was going to order a small cheese pizza until Lottie's mom said she was paying. Maria switched her order. Large pizza with all kinds of toppings, much more than she could ever eat. I thought she would take home the rest, but she didn't. She didn't pay for the pizza so she could waste it."

"You want to pay for your lessons, so you won't waste them?"

"That's part of it. I think I might try a little harder, practice a little more if I'm paying. I think people are like that."

"No one ever washes a rental car."

"What?"

"Your father used to tell me that. What people don't own, they don't take care of. Why would they?

They don't get any benefit from spending money on what someone else owns. What people own, what they've paid for, they maintain. It's part of our system."

"I never thought of it like that. Still, I want to pay for my lessons. Then, if I don't like singing, I won't feel so bad about quitting."

Hope hugged her daughter. "We'll find you a job, and you can help with your lessons. For right now, we'll simply keep a ledger of what they cost. Then, when you make a million dollars, you can repay me."

"No problem, Mom. I'll even buy you a new car."

"Great, a BMW?"

"I was thinking some kind of small Chevy."

"Your generosity is a little underwhelming."

"No one ever washes a rental car."

Hope laughed, and Cori laughed with her.

That night, before she went to bed, Hope stopped in the attic office to say goodnight to Max. She found him staring at the computer, just staring.

"Something wrong, Max?"

He turned to her. "The IRS, the Internal Revenue Service, wishes to speak with me."

4

Hope laughed. "The IRS? How in the world did you manage to get on their radar?"

"It's my own fault, Mrs. Herring. I was surfing the net, as the saying goes, and I reached a site that asked for a social security number. There was no social security when I was alive, so I never acquired a number. As a ghost, I could hardly expect anything to come of keying in a made-up number. Didn't seem too difficult. I'm still not well-read on the ins and outs of the social security system. In any case, my fake number was reported to the IRS, and now, they wish to interview me."

"That isn't possible. Yet, if you tell them the truth, they won't believe you."

"I don't see where it's possible to reveal the truth.

I mean, I could chat with someone on the phone or over the Internet, even through email or snail mail, as many users call the postal system. However, that would open a can of worms. I can't give them my true birth date, as that would make me the oldest human on the planet. No one is going to believe that."

"Are there penalties for using a bogus number?" Hope asked.

"I looked it up. Actually, using someone else's number is a federal offense. The maximum penalty is fifteen years in federal prison."

"That sounds serious. I take it they know your real name?"

"In that reference, I have the upper hand. I used my real first name but not my real surname." Max smiled. "I was not an utter fool."

"Perhaps not, but did you use your correct address?"

He frowned. "I suppose they do have that."

"I'm guessing they might be able to harvest a good deal of information about you and your Internet habits. Of course, they have no idea that you don't really exist."

"I don't?" Max looked surprised.

"Not in a corporeal form. They're looking for a live person. You know what I mean."

"I do indeed. What tack do I take to rid myself of this particular problem?"

"The truth won't suffice. One, they won't believe you. Two, telling a lie to them is probably also against the law."

"They hold all the aces, don't they?"

"I wouldn't go that far. We might have to think about this one for a while. As of right now, it's obvious that you won't talk to anyone from the IRS. Not online or off. As far as they're concerned, you don't exist. Simply ignore any more messages."

"What if they come looking?"

"I'm inclined to tell them that I created your character, and I messed up when I put in a fake social security number."

"What if they don't like that answer?"

"I doubt they will do anything but slap my wrist and make me promise not to do it again. But, no one will knock on the door. It's not like you made a bunch of money that they want to tax."

"You know, the income tax was a novelty when I was alive. It applied to very few people, and the tax was quite small."

"Let's not worry about the IRS. I think they have

better things to do than chase down someone using a fake SSN, especially since you're not employed or earning money."

Max made eye contact with Hope. "I have considered finding a job of some sort."

"You, too?"

"What do you know about gig work? I'm certain it does not entail actually gigging, which we did with frogs when I was young."

"Nowadays, a gig is a one-time job. Musicians, especially small bands, use the term for a job that might last a weekend. There are no long-term contracts. You might have considered them day labor."

"Ah, yes, I understand. There was an empty lot where men and some women would gather. If you needed someone to paint a room or a door or help with a fence or barn, you could stop and hire what you needed. It was an efficient way to hire help without committing to employment."

"Gig work is efficient, for everyone involved. Since it sometimes involves cash, the government doesn't like it much. It's hard to verify cash transactions, so they can be properly taxed."

"An infernal problem when I was alive also. Gig

work online? That seems to be the only gig work I might be able to obtain."

"Gig work is popular over the Internet, but it is cashless. Payment is wired from one account to the other. So, there is always a record of what you've earned."

"So, the IRS can come after you."

"Exactly. Max, you have no reason to earn money. You have no needs."

"But, you do, Mrs. Herring. I would like to contribute to the upkeep of this house."

"You repay me by seeing to our security. You provide a valuable service that I would have to pay for otherwise."

"I am aware of that. Still, I would like to do more."

"Perhaps, we can set it up that you do the work, and the earnings go to Cori. How would that sound?"

"Capital idea, Mrs. Herring. She has a social security number, I take it?"

"She does. You would be contributing to her voice lessons and music study."

"Then, it is simply a matter of finding gigs. I shall look into it right away."

"Before you sign up for anything, I'll need to make sure it's okay with Cori."

"I trust your powers of persuasion. This is the purpose I've been looking for. You are a lifesaver. Well, a ghost saver, anyway."

Hope laughed. "Goodnight, Max."

In bed, Hope wondered just what Max might be able to do. Did he have a skill or talent that people were willing to pay for? She supposed he did, although she wasn't sure where he might find his niche. She was pretty sure Cori would welcome Max's support. After all, Max didn't need any money.

The next morning, Hope floated the idea past Cori, who was more than willing to accept help from Max. Bijou sat in the chair next to Cori and the teen ran her hand over the soft fur.

"You'll have to open a bank account, so his earnings can go straight to the bank."

"I already have an account."

"You can't use that. I don't think it's a good idea to comingle what you have with what he'll add. In fact, I don't think you should put your earnings in the account you already have. You don't want someone thinking that what you have already saved should be taxed."

"They can do that?"

"The government can do a lot of things. Keeping everything clean is best for everyone."

"Roger that."

Before classes started, Hope found an email from Brad. It provided the details for Cori's lessons. One hour because he had found that students lost focus after that. Daily practice, because every day Cori didn't practice was another day before she became great. Thursdays after school would be the best time. Mondays and Fridays were too close to the weekend, and he thought Thursday was a lackluster day. Cori would have something to look forward to. Besides, there weren't many school holidays on Thursdays. He quoted a price that seemed reasonable, and he said lessons would be in his house. He had a piano, and it was safe from prying eyes and ears. Cori didn't yet need an audience.

Hope checked off all the items and sent a quick acceptance. The lessons would start in one week. That would give everyone a chance to work out the schedule. She didn't inform Cori, as Cori didn't need a distraction while she was at school. After classes would be soon enough.

As Hope walked to her SUV, she noticed Walter Zalar standing next to Virginia's sporty, red Tesla. Bald and paunchy, Walt was older than Virginia and looked it. His face was pale, and to Hope's eyes, his hands trembled slightly. She didn't remember that about him, but then, she had met him only once or twice. He always stood behind Virginia, who was the more vocal of the two.

"Walt," Hope called out, "looking for Virginia?"

He smiled a pained smile, as if he had some affliction. "She's coming. She just texted me. Say, can I ask you a question?"

"Sure." Hope veered closer. "What's on your mind?"

"You're known for solving murders, correct?"

"I've helped law enforcement a few times. They did all the real work."

"Exactly. I figured as much. You don't help with open and shut cases, do you?"

"Open and shut?" Hope tilted her head slightly to the side.

"You know, someone tries to rob a convenience store, and the clerk shoots the robber. Nothing there to solve, right?" Walt suggested.

"I wouldn't get involved in something like that. Why do you ask?"

"Oh, I have a brother in California. Someone broke into his apartment while he was sleeping. My brother shot the intruder, killing him. The police didn't arrest him. No one filed charges. Yet, the family of the intruder is suing. How can that happen?"

"I'm no attorney, but I think that even without criminal charges, people can initiate a wrongful death suit. Think of doctors whose patients die. Might not be murder, but it could still pay out a lot of insurance money."

"Yes, I see that. That makes sense. So, you wouldn't be interested in a case like that?"

"No, that's not really in my lane. The facts are well known, and they'll determine the outcome. Tell your brother to trust the police, who generally do a great job of obtaining facts."

"Will do. Thanks, Hope. I will tell you that I've always been one of your fans. Not that I keep up on things. I love the idea of amateur detectives. I used to read mysteries all the time. They could do so much." Walt smiled.

"They're called amateurs for a reason," Hope told him. "I think the police procedural has replaced the amateurs of old. There's simply too much science involved. Individuals don't have access to all that lab work."

"I agree. Oh, here she comes. Thanks again."

Hope watched as Walt moved off to hug his wife.

It was a warm gesture that made Hope smile. To her way of thinking, it was living proof that a difference in age didn't always pose a problem.

"That's great," Cori said after meeting her mother by the SUV and reading the email Brad had sent to Hope. "I can't wait."

"I'm guessing that Lottie will want to go with you sometimes," Hope said, "but I don't think that's a good idea."

"I'm not taking her. She would become a distraction because when she's not the center of attention, she acts out. I don't need that. I'm pretty sure Mr. Edie doesn't need it either."

"Good call. I'll remind you that you have to practice every day. That includes weekends and holidays. I suggest you choose a time, either morning or evening, when you can practice. If you set a time, you're more likely to do the task."

"Like setting an alarm?"

"Much like that. Most nights, I don't use an alarm. I wake up about the same time every morning."

"Oh, gosh, I don't want that to happen to me. I like to sleep too much."

Hope chuckled. "At your age, you don't have to worry about it. When you get older, it just happens, although I think it's the result of reduced bladder size."

"That's another thing I don't want to know about."

"Growing old is not for sissies, as the saying goes."

"I'll take my time, if you don't mind."

Max waited in the kitchen. He wore a tan suit, a blue shirt, and a red and navy striped tie. He looked thoroughly businesslike.

"My, my," Hope said, "what's the occasion?"

"My first gig," Max answered. "I am to proofread a two-hundred-page book, a novel, I believe. I want to feel like I'm working again."

"Super," Cori said. "I'm guessing there's not a lot of money involved, and that's just fine, as I don't yet have a bank account."

"Tomorrow we'll get you one. I suppose you have a few days to finish, Max?"

"One week, Mrs. Herring. I am certain I can meet my deadline, although I am not as well versed in word processors as I wish to be."

"Cori can help," Hope said, "since she's going to benefit from your work."

"Sure, Max," Cori said. "As soon as I finish my homework."

"I'll be in the attic," Max told her with a grin.

Hope watched Cori leave and Max disappear. She wondered about the different ways something could go wrong.

Only about a thousand popped into her head.

The real question was which one would arrive first.

5

Hope arrived at school early enough to visit Brad in the music room. He was sipping coffee and staring at a desktop filled with brass trumpet parts.

"Good morning," he said and pointed at the parts. "This is what happens when you don't put it back together before you leave for the day."

"Stuck?"

"No, just tired. Some mornings are worse than others."

"Don't I know it. You got my email?"

"I did, and thanks. I hope Cori is looking forward to her lessons."

"She is. I've tried to impress upon her the need for practice, but I'm not sure it took."

"She'll be fine. I believe in just the right amount

of practice. We don't want to strain vocal cords through overuse."

"I agree. Please make sure she understands that. There is such a thing as over-practice, right?"

"There is when muscles are concerned. Don't worry, Hope. She'll do fine. I hope you will too."

At that moment, a man walked into the room. He was fit and well-dressed but not as handsome as Brad.

"Oh, you're busy," the man said.

"No, he's not," Hope said. "I'm on my way out."

"Hope, this is Chuck, a friend of mine."

Chuck extended his hand, and Hope shook it. Chuck had gray eyes and a large nose.

"Glad to meet you," Chuck said. "You're a teacher here?"

"I am," Hope answered, "which is why I have to be going." She waved to Brad. "Thursday."

"Wait, is there anything Cori is allergic to? I would hate to feed her some snack that's going to cause a problem."

"Sometimes, I think she's allergic to hard work, but that's how most parents feel. No allergies. Nice meeting you, Chuck."

Hope left, glancing once over her shoulder and

spotting the two men smiling warmly at one another.

When Hope entered her classroom, she found John Hittle waiting for her. Short and stocky with a buzz haircut, John taught social studies. Hope had never had many dealings with him, but the word in the teachers' lounge was that he adhered to a dated and strict view of proper decorum. Wearing a starched shirt, tie, and cuffed pants, all he needed was a Bible to pass for a preacher. She was pretty sure he did give a sermon once in a while.

"Mrs. Herring, glad I caught you. The students will arrive soon, so I'll make this brief. My church is sponsoring a Bible studies club here at the school. It's not much. Once a month, interested students will get together and review a Biblical text. We believe there is much to learn from the good book. Attendance is strictly voluntary. At the end of the year, there will be some sort of field trip. There are no plans for that yet. I was wondering if you would be interested in joining and perhaps, leading the discussion on occasion."

Hope smiled and shook her head. "I appreciate the offer, but I don't think that's for me."

"You don't believe in the Bible?" the man asked.

"It's not that. I think religion is personal. People should form their own connections."

"That's quite all right, although I might warn you that there are teachers in this school who might be grooming children."

"Grooming?"

"You know, turning them to the dark side. I won't name names. I think we all know who these teachers are. A Bible studies group would be a good counterbalance."

"I am a live-and-let-live type of person. If there's something improper going on, you should take it to the principal."

"I have, and I will continue to do so. You know, evil thrives when good people do nothing."

With a tight smile, John turned and walked out. Hope stared for a moment. She had no idea who might be "grooming" students. She didn't want to know. Knowing meant she would have to do something. In this case, it was better to be ignorant. Luckily, her students streamed into the room and grabbed her attention. She forgot all about John, especially later in the day when she found Max in the attic office, staring at his computer screen.

"Mrs. Herring," Max said, "do the schools not teach basic English these days?"

"What do you mean?" she asked, setting her briefcase down next to the desk.

"This book I am editing breaks every rule of English that I know of. You would think the basics of syntax, subject-verb agreement, tenses, and proper nouns would have been memorized by any would-be author."

"Problems?"

"'Problems' doesn't begin to describe this manuscript. It is hardly readable. The spelling is mostly correct, which tells me the writer used spellcheck. Unfortunately, a good editing app was not used."

"I'm sure you'll be able to make it better."

"At the cost of rewriting most of the paragraphs and sentences. How anyone could have graduated from high school with these atrocious habits is beyond me. I am about to pull out my hair. Wait, I can't do that, but you know what I mean."

"I always try to remember that the point of writing is to communicate. If the writer manages to do that, then breaking a few English conventions isn't a big deal."

"I agree, but most conventions were invented in order to enhance communication. They are not arbitrary notions scribbled on the blackboard by some scolding schoolmarm."

"I'm sure you'll be able to add coherence to the work."

Max shrugged. "I should have charged double what I'm being paid."

"You had the low bid?"

"I must have. I've taken the time to work out my hourly rate, and I can assure you that it is far below minimum wage."

"Perhaps, you need to sharpen your bidding skills."

"Indeed. I am fortunate that I don't have to sleep. If I did, I would never finish this gig on time."

"Live and learn, Max. Live and learn."

"If I weren't doing this for Cori, I would have quit hours ago."

"Don't do it for her. Do it because you enjoy the work."

"Hah! I will enjoy the work when I don't have to change every fourth word ... and yes, I kept count."

Hope laughed.

"Stay out of Max's way," Hope told Cori over dinner. "He's in the throes of editing a book that needs much more than editing."

"A total rewrite? How did he manage to get himself into that?"

"A poor bid on gig work. Let this be a lesson for us. Don't leap into some job until you know the extent of the work involved. Sometimes, the pay doesn't match the effort."

"A teachable moment. I'll go up to the attic later and offer him some encouragement."

"Good idea. Ready for your upcoming lesson?"

"I've been thinking, maybe, I shouldn't take voice lessons. What if I'm not good enough? I will have wasted time and effort."

"Self-doubt is the bane of procrastinators. Try it anyway. You know about Thomas Edison, don't you?"

"The guy who invented, like, a thousand things? Yeah, I've heard about him."

"Yes, well, he would run the same experiment over and over. Why? Because he learned from each iteration. Learning what doesn't work is sometimes as valuable as learning what does."

"Are you sure about that?" Cori gave her mother a quizzical look.

"Absolutely, but don't make the mistake of trying out all the experiments that others have already performed. Your goal is to learn from those trials and expand upon them. No one needs to reinvent the wheel."

Cori laughed. "No, they just reinvent versions of the wheel."

"Exactly. So, assume you're going to love voice lessons. You're going to love performing. You're going to learn a great deal about yourself and your grit."

"Grit? What do you mean?"

"George W. Cecil said, 'On the plains of hesitation bleach the bones of countless millions who, at the dawn of indecision, sat down to wait, and waiting died.'"

"Wow, you memorized that? Why?"

"Because victory always comes with a price. Very few people win on the first try. More people fail because they don't finish what they started ... the plains of hesitation. Some people are afraid of winning. Don't ask me why. I don't know. But, they are. I read once about a female professional golfer who lost tournaments on purpose when she was a teenager."

"Why would she do that?'

"She was afraid of public speaking. She didn't want to have to talk to the crowd."

"She tanked to avoid a speech?"

"So it would seem."

"That's crazy."

"Not for some people. I think that if you research 'stage fright' on the Internet, you will find that more than a few very good performers were scared to death before they faced the audience. I believe there is a bit of that in almost everyone. No one wants to get booed."

Cori bit her lip a moment. "I have a question. How do you know if you're good?"

"Good?"

"You know, if you sing well or act well or play sports well. How do you know if you're good?"

"Competition. If you're serious about doing something, really doing something, then you have to compete. It's that simple. You are judged by whomever else is doing what you're doing. You compete against another human, not a robot."

"In chess, I'm always competing against a bot."

"On the computer, but in matches, you face another person across the board. You don't have to be the best chess player in the world. You simply have to be better than your opponent."

"That's how I'll know if I'm good? If I can beat the other person? That's not much of a bar to jump over. It's like playing darts against a blind person."

"I think that if you search, you will find some expert, blind dart throwers."

"You're joking."

"It really isn't all that difficult when you think about it. The dart board is a certain height, and it's a specified distance away. A blind person, with someone chasing down the darts, would be able to become quite proficient. Doesn't Lottie have a dart board in her basement? You might try it sometime."

"All right, I'll give you the dart thing, but bad analogy. Back to singing. How will I know that I'm good? When I can win some sort of sing-off?"

"Basically, you don't have to win a contest. You can use a proxy, like your record sales. If people buy your recordings, then you're good. If you go on social media and gather a couple million followers, then you must be good."

"Or you're terrible. I know some people online who are so bad they get followed."

"True. Either end of the spectrum might work, but the people in the middle won't make the big time."

"They give up?"

"Some do. Some become satisfied with what they can do. Think of sports. There are a bunch of girls and boys who play sports in elementary school. A smaller group plays in high school. College sports are the home of the best high schoolers. Professional sports glean the best from the colleges. Now, at some point, every person trying to join the professional ranks reached a fork in the road. One side went to the next level, the other went off the sports road and into something else. At that fork, a person examines his or her performance. Most will admit that they simply aren't good enough for the professional road. No amount of work or grit will make up for the lack of skill and talent so you walk the other fork in the road."

"That's giving up."

"In a way, it is, but it's not really. It's coming to the realization that you're never going to be good enough in that particular field. You're the really short person trying to play professional basketball."

Cori laughed. "Don't they have a pro league for petite people?"

"You know what I mean. Besides recognizing your limits is a good thing. In a world of limited time, you shouldn't waste yours on something that can't happen or that you don't enjoy. There might be blind dart throwers, but I don't think there are blind race car drivers."

"Yeah, that would be crazy."

"Trust me, Cori, you'll know when you're good and when you're not good. Although, it helps to have someone you trust give you an honest opinion."

"Mr. Edie?"

"Yep, he'll do for now."

Before bed, Hope visited Max one more time. He was dressed as an old-time accountant—green eyeshade, sleeve protectors with garters, round spectacles, white shirt, and black tie.

"Does the costume help?" Hope asked the ghost.

"I believe so, Mrs. Herring. I have settled into a sort of rhythm. By morning, I hope to have ten percent of the book corrected."

"Good for you."

"Oh, by the way, I received a second missive from the IRS."

"And?"

"And, I ignored it. I don't exist, right?"

"Let's hope they soon realize that." But a shiver of worry ran down Hope's spine.

6

By the time Thursday arrived, Hope could tell that Max was in a decided funk. She found him staring at the computer still wearing his accountant uniform, but he was no longer typing like a court reporter. Bijou sat on the desk next to the computer watching the ghost.

"Something wrong, Max?" Hope asked.

"Just taking a brief respite, Mrs. Herring."

He turned, and she could swear he had circles under his eyes, which was impossible. He was a ghost. They never changed.

"No, that's not quite the truth," he continued. "I have run out of energy. Well, that's not the truth either. I have become discouraged. That is the truth.

I can see the light at the end of the tunnel, but it may well be an approaching train."

"What's gone wrong?" Hope sat in the chair next to him.

"I sent my employer the first part of the rewrite, and while she was encouraging for the most part, she deemed my prose old and no longer in use. I admit I used some words and phrases from my own era, but I hardly wrote in some ancient language."

"Specifically?"

"She contended that I write too many complete sentences. Mrs. Herring, I was taught to write sentences, not parts of sentences nor one-word paragraphs. Sentences, perfectly good, subject-verb-object sentences. She believes I need to put more variety in my prose. I tried to inform her that I was not trying to create a new style. I was trying to communicate."

"I would tell you that monotony is the enemy of book reading, but I'm sure you understand that. However, you might try to create different rhythms. Some long sentences, some shorter ones, but I'm not one to lecture anyone on writing."

"No, no, you're right. I do have a tendency to obey all the little rules I was taught. Great writers don't worry about those, do they?"

"I wouldn't know, Max." Hope grinned. "I'm not a great writer."

The ghost laughed. "Apparently, neither am I, and now, I must return to my work. My moment of self-pity is over. I have promised to finish this by Sunday, and I will manage that. I have forgotten ... is this Cori's first voice lesson day?"

"It is. I'll be taking her in a few minutes. She's excited, as you might guess. I'm sure in a few weeks, she might not be so enthused."

"Work is work. I have always known that, but my decades away from work spoiled me. When I was alive, I would hire people who would work no matter how they felt. Most people can't force themselves to do something they despise. Successful people have a way of focusing on the work and on what has to be done. The work may be boring, but it has to be done."

"You'll do fine, Max. People eat an elephant one bite at a time."

The ghost's shoulders sagged. "This is more like a dinosaur."

When Hope entered the kitchen, she found Cori there tapping on her phone.

"Ready?" Hope asked.

"Aren't we going to be early?"

"Yes, but Mr. Edie has promised to give me a tour of his place."

"A tour?"

"You're still my responsibility. If you think I'm going to send you into someone's loft without checking it out, you don't know your mother."

Cori rolled her blue eyes. "When are you going to let me grow up?"

"Never. I'll be your mother till the day I am no longer on this planet. Get used to it. Although, I'm certain that at some point you'll no longer be around for me to steer."

"We're both looking forward to that day."

"Hush and brush your teeth."

"Huh?"

"You're taking voice lessons. You don't want your breath to smell like a Tennessee billy goat."

"Have you ever really smelled a billy goat from Tennessee?"

"That's not the issue. I'm sure they smell perfectly horrid. Teeth."

Cori walked out, and Hope asked herself if she was too controlling. Parenting was always a battle about control. How much was too much? How much was too little? She wasn't Goldilocks. She wasn't going to get it just right every time. Maybe never.

Hope sighed. Was the joy Cori brought worth the consternation?

Yes, it sure was.

Brad's "loft" was a smallish, light yellow stucco house on the edge of town with a neat, trimmed lawn, a roof streaked by runoff, and gorgeous landscaping with climbing ivy and flowering bushes all around the yard. There were a number of pine trees behind the house, which made it typical. Pine trees were a staple in North Carolina.

"It almost looks like a hobbit house," Cori remarked with a smile.

"I think it's really charming." Hope admired the plants blooming near the house.

Brad's SUV was parked in the driveway, and he answered on the first knock. Apparently, the doorbell no longer functioned.

"You need a new doorbell," Cori said as she passed the man. Brad chuckled.

"I need a lot of things," he answered.

The house had been converted into a sort of studio. In the main room, there was a piano and huge TV. The kitchen was modern enough, but it wasn't exactly a gourmet's hideaway. One bedroom had been converted into a music room. It was padded and contained music stands and amps, as well as guitars and two saxophones.

"The loud instruments are taught in here," Brad explained. "I don't have a lot of neighbors, but I don't want complaints especially since some of my students don't create anything close to music."

"Voice?" Hope asked.

"Not usually. Voices aren't so loud. That's generally done at the piano."

"Why do you call this the loft?" Cori asked. "I don't see a loft."

Brad smiled. "This way."

A flight of narrow stairs led to the attic. Cori was the first to enter the space, and she just stopped and stared.

The room had been transformed into a recording studio. There was the soundproof room where the recording was done, a mixing table where someone could add and subtract tracks in order to smooth a sound, mics, headphones, and comfy, leather chairs. Hope knew that many a rainy afternoon was spent turning out music in here.

"Impressive," Hope said, turning in a small circle.

"This is my baby," Brad answered. "I can do almost everything a big studio can do. I would tell you how much all this cost, but I'm ashamed. No one should sink so much money into something that doesn't offer a return on investment. Take a good look, Cori. This is the reason I not only teach in school, but I do private lessons too. I'm poor because of my crazy hobby."

"It's cool," Cori said. "Can I make a recording some day?"

"Sure. In fact, we'll probably do one the next time you come. I'd like to get your voice on tape, so we can gauge your progress. How does that sound?"

"Very cool." Cori's eyes shone.

Hope, too, was impressed. "I can see why you could spend a lot of time up here."

"I hate to admit this, but I have some friends that are musicians. We do small gigs around the state, and we record sometimes. I don't do vocals, just guitar and sax. It's another source of income, although it doesn't pay much. We do it just because we love to perform. I tell you what. One of these weekends, I'll invite you to come watch."

"Me?" Cori asked.

"You," he replied. "Ninety-nine percent of all musicians play for the love of what they do and the peanuts they might earn. Modern sound systems can make almost anyone sound good. Some people think that someday, there will be no more human musicians. We'll have bots that can play any instrument expertly. Bots will never miss a note or nuance, and they'll work for next to nothing. They won't get sick, and they won't lose their voices."

"Won't the music sound like bot music?" Hope asked.

"Yes, I suspect that some of the creativity will be lost. Well, delayed. A bot might be able to race through so many different riffs that finding the right one will be inevitable. All that's needed is a producer with a good ear."

"I don't know if I would like that," Cori said.

"Sound is sound," Brad said. "Whatever a human can create, a bot can mimic, but I don't think human musicians will ever become obsolete. We need the emotion, the uniqueness that a living being brings."

Hope left the loft and the house, promising to come back in an hour and collect her daughter. She drove to the Lost Volume Book Store. The bookstore was not part of any chain, even though it was new. Located on a side street downtown, it catered to locals who wanted to get away from the fray. People came and browsed the books, often finding something in the "used" section that would be fun for an hour or two. The owners, a couple from India, were always around and always helpful.

She bought a cup of coffee and settled in an overstuffed chair before she pulled out her phone and paged through her email. The walls of books reminded Hope of the stacks in the college library. When she needed to study or write a paper, she would delve deep into the stacks and find an isolated table or desk. The stacks were quiet, almost scary. Occasionally, she would feel that someone was watching her, perhaps peeking between the books. That was creepy. When it happened, she generally packed up her papers and books and left.

Lost Volume never felt like that. It was more nest than stacks.

As Hope waded through her junk mail, she wondered why some emails never disappeared. She deleted the items without reading them. She never replied. Why did the sender continue to fill her inbox? Oh, she knew it wasn't really a sender. Someone created a short message and, with one tap on the keyboard, sent it to a million addresses. It didn't cost much more to send it to ten million people than to send it to a single person. If the service were a flat rate, then every additional address lowered the cost per person. Who wouldn't advertise that way? Still, she would think that sooner or later the sender would scrub the list and get rid of people who never opened the emails.

Hope waited a full hour before she returned to Brad's house. She found Brad and Cori at the piano where he was still tuning her voice. He would play a note, and she would try to produce the same pitch.

"She's a natural," Brad said, "and, I'm not saying that because you're paying me. Cori needs some refinement, and I'll teach her to read music better."

"I'm just learning," Cori said in her defense. "I'll get better."

"I'm sure you will. See you Saturday night," Brad told them.

"What?" Hope asked. "What's Saturday?"

Brad grinned. "My band has a gig just outside of town. It's at a small pub called The Fancy Dan. The first session starts at eight. I'll introduce you to the band, and Cori can experience what it's like to play in tiny places for people who might not exactly love the music."

"A honkytonk?" Hope asked.

"Something like that. Not to worry though. The owner has a firm hand and a big bouncer. Things won't get rowdy."

"They better not."

A light rain started as Hope drove home. "Did you like it?" she asked.

"I did," Cori answered. "I wasn't sure I was going to, but I do. I like it. Mr. Edie didn't mess around. As soon as you left, we started the lesson, and we didn't take a break. I have some drills I need to do, but not tonight. Voices, like all muscles, need time to recover."

"So, we come back next week?"

"We do. Want to know something funny? His bathroom smells like perfume. I hate to admit it, but I found some in the cabinet under the sink."

"Just because he's a man doesn't mean he can't appreciate good smells."

Cori frowned. "You mean ... his partner?"

"It wouldn't surprise me. I would think he would appreciate a partner who didn't smell like—

"A Tennessee billy goat," Cori finished.

Hope laughed. "Exactly. You're old enough to understand fragrances. Do you have a favorite?"

"Not yet, Mom. I'm not really interested in that."

Hope glanced over and wondered how much she didn't know about her daughter. Perfume might be something that Cori would soon embrace, or never like. Another choice in growing up.

When Hope walked into her house, she found

Max moving around the living room and Bijou watching him.

"What are you doing?" Cori asked.

"A dance," Max replied, "something we did when I was young."

"Why?" Hope asked.

"The IRS sent another email."

7

Hope frowned. "You're dancing because the IRS sent an email?"

"Exactly."

"May I ask why?"

"Because I looked up the IRS online, and I discovered that they don't use email. They send letters. So, the email I received was a fake, Mrs. Herring. This second email confirms that. I am not being investigated by the IRS. So ... I'm dancing ... with joy."

Bijou trilled.

"Good for you. That is a reason to celebrate. You avoided a scam."

"I have indeed. I know this looks a bit unconstrained, but I had to do something."

"Keep dancing. I have to make dinner."

Hope had just started boiling the noodles when Cori entered the kitchen.

"Did you notice Max?" Cori asked.

"Who could have missed that?"

"Why is he so happy?"

"The IRS is not after him. It was a scam."

"Cool, but that's still a weird dance."

"They danced differently in his time. I'm sure that if you looked at the dances I used to do, you'd find them weird, too. But then, I find break dancing and some other stuff pretty strange."

"I suppose people dance just because it makes them feel good."

"That's par for the course. Joy brings energy, and energy wants to be used."

"When will dinner be ready?"

"Thirty minutes."

"I'll be back. I want to practice a little."

"Not too much though."

"No, Mom, Mr. Edie already warned me."

Hope continued with dinner, wondering about her daughter and her dedication to singing. Hope knew that, more than likely, Cori would end up saddened and discouraged. Yet, that would be a good lesson. Cori would discover that she could fail at something and move on. People failed all the time. It was part of growing up. It was part of life. Failure was the human condition. Steam rose from the boiling water and disappeared. Hot turned to cold.

The Fancy Dan was anything but fancy. The tavern sat by itself twelve miles outside of Castle Park and had a gravel lot where cars were parked at all angles as if the customers had arrived drunk. Hope managed to find a spot where she would be certain to be able to leave. The last thing she wanted was to be boxed in.

"What's Fancy An mean?" Cori asked looking at the sign.

"It's Fancy Dan," Hope answered. "The D has lost its neon or something."

"Okay, so what does Fancy Dan mean?"

"It's an old expression. It meant someone who put on fancy clothes or had a flamboyant way of acting. You might call a high-end restaurant a fancy dan."

Cori chuckled. "This is no high-end restaurant."

"No, it's closer to a honkytonk, and if you want to know what that means, look it up. You have a phone."

"I know what a honkytonk is ... I think."

"Yes, well, you'll probably see and hear some things

that are not exactly polite. That's what happens in these places. It's early by honkytonk hours so there shouldn't be any problems. If there are, we leave, got that?"

With a frown, Cori said, "Yes, Mom."

"Let's not get separated. If you have to use the restroom, and I don't think you'll find it terribly clean, I'll go with you. I'm guessing it will be mostly dark inside, although there won't be any smoking, as that's against the law in North Carolina."

"I know how to act. I'm not going to run off to the dance floor."

"I don't know if there will be a dance floor. We're here to watch the band. Remember that."

"I won't forget."

The tavern was half full. Hope and Cori waited by the door. To one side were pool tables and dart boards. A long bar ran down the other side, and its stools were mostly taken. Any number of colorful neon signs were hung over the back bar. It seemed every brewer in the country had contributed something. The two bartenders kept busy while several waitresses stood at one end, waiting for the drinks.

The stage stood in the far corner. It was filled with drums and instruments, telling Hope that Brad and his band had already set up. The Fancy Dan was exactly what Hope remembered from her college years ... pitchers of beer, cardboard pizza, and loud music. Some things never changed.

"There you are."

Hope turned to the voice as Brad stepped forward to hug her and Cori.

"I'm so glad you made it," he continued. "Come on, I got you a table."

Hope followed Brad across the room to a small table set against a wall to one side of the stage.

"Here you go. Have a seat. What are you drinking?"

"One beer," Hope said.

"Bottled water," Cori added.

"I'll be right back."

From the table, Hope could see both the band and the audience, and she supposed Brad wanted it that way. She was glad that they weren't set out in front, where they would be noticed.

"What do you think?" Hope asked.

"It's like a movie," Cori said. "Not too clean and smells like sweaty people."

"You got it. We'll stay through the first set, then we'll go home."

"Roger that."

Brad arrived with their drinks and a red, plastic basket filled with popcorn.

"This is the best food in the place," he said and sat. "We're getting ready to start, so I'll make this quick. I don't anticipate any trouble tonight. That doesn't mean there won't be some. Men and women drinking hard sometimes don't see eye to eye. In any case, there's an exit four steps that way." He pointed. "That's the quickest way out. I know it says for emergencies only, but ignore that. Just get out and keep going."

"You've played here before?"

He nodded. "No problems, but you never know."

"Is this the worst place you've played?" Cori asked.

Brad laughed. "Not by a long shot. This is somewhere in the middle. We have a sort of clientele here. People come to hear us play. There will be some dancing in the aisles, but that's not an issue."

A woman roughly Hope's age dressed in leather pants, boots, and a leather bustier, stepped onto the stage.

"Who's that?" Cori asked.

"That's Wanda, not her real name. She's our vocalist. She does most of the singing, but we all act as a chorus. She's good, and she's been doing this for a while. Not for the money, because there isn't much of that. She sings because she loves to sing for an audience. Don't mind the outfit. She's working for tips."

"Has she been singing for a long time?"

"Yes, a lot like you, she started in school, then college. She did some singing in Raleigh and Atlanta, but never got that break. She has a husband and kids, and she still loves to sing. I gotta run. We'll be starting soon."

Brad left for the stage, and Hope turned to Cori. "What are you thinking?"

Cori frowned. "She started out just like me."

"No, not exactly. You're not her and you never will be, no matter how your singing works out."

"Yeah."

A few minutes later, Brad and the band took the stage. They paid no attention to the people playing pool or the ones eating. They launched into a well-known song and kept at it. Halfway through, Wanda stepped to the mic and sang. While the noise and acoustics distorted the sound, Hope could tell that Wanda possessed a good voice, not concert quality, maybe, but definitely good.

"She can sing," Cori said when the song ended.

"She's had lots of practice," Hope replied. "She's a good performer."

"Yeah, and it shows."

The entire band was good, and occasionally, one of the musicians would do a solo riff. If they missed a note or chord here and there, Hope couldn't tell. Her ear wasn't attuned to the music. She thought they sounded very professional, which was the goal. They displayed a high level of skill.

Toward the end of the set, Wanda left the band and came over to the table. As soon as she sat, a waitress placed a drink in front of her.

"How do you like it?" Wanda asked.

"You sound great," Cori answered.

"Good equipment makes all the difference. I can hear the mistakes, but the people in the audience can't."

"Is it always like this?"

"Yes and no," Wanda said. "Some nights are more crowded than others. Some nights are noisier, but those are little differences. What you see is what you get on any given night. The tattoos and blue jeans change, but the attitudes don't. I've seen it rowdier, but I've never seen it as quiet as a concert hall. That doesn't happen."

"Can I ask a question?"

"Sure, Cori, ask away."

"Why do you do this?"

Wanda smiled. "Honestly? I do it because I can. I'm still young enough to have a voice, and this place has the right feel for a singer like me. The money, well, the money isn't much at all. It hardly covers gas, but I'm not working for free so that's a good thing. You would not believe how many singers work for free. They're desperate to perform." She stopped and stared at the band for a moment. "I'll be honest with you. I'm here because I love to sing. I'm not talking about echoes in the shower or church singing. I'm talking about performing. I love it. I don't much care if the audience goes ga-ga over me. As long as they don't drown me out or throw beer bottles at me, I'm fine. Just let me do the songs and applaud at appropriate times. That's why I'm here. I love it."

"How long have you been doing it?"

Wanda shrugged. "A long time. I started younger than you are now. I sang in church and at all the school shows. I was the soloist. The bright lights blinded me early. When I was a teenager, I had a chance to go on tour with a good band that opened for a better band. I was about to take the job when another singer, an older singer, talked to me. She said that if I had the chance, I should go to college. A degree in my pocket was a bargaining chip. I wouldn't need to sing in order to eat. She was a backup singer, and she said she wished she had a degree. She was never going to be a lead. It was that simple. Like any job, backup was tedious."

"What did you major in?" Hope asked.

"Music and education, like Brad.

"So, you teach?"

"I have a teacher's license, and that's my day job. It's a good job. I have a nice family. There are times I ask myself why I didn't go touring as a teenager. I thought I could be one of those one-name singers that you see in music videos. I might have made it. I don't know."

"So, you're telling me not to try to be a star?" Cori asked.

"No, no, I would never discourage you. It wasn't in the cards for me, but that doesn't mean it can't work for you. I went to the University of North Carolina in Chapel Hill. I was Eponine in Les Miz. I was good, but the girl who played Fantine was better. I was pretty proud of myself, but I could tell she sang circles around me. She was the real deal. At the end of the semester, she left. She had a contract with some music producer. She made some recordings.

She was on a couple of TV talent shows. For a couple of years, she was right there on the edge of stardom. The right break, and she would have been on easy street. That break never came. Then the phone didn't ring as often. She couldn't act, although she tried. She disappeared."

"Did she finish school?"

Wanda shook her head. "No, she took to drugs and booze. If you learn anything tonight, learn to stay away from those two little things. They don't help, not ever. Anyway, she wound her way through rehabs until she managed to control her urges. She no longer sings. She lives in Florida where she sells real estate and takes care of her children. I believe she's happy."

"You kept up with her?" Hope asked.

Wanda smiled. "I did. I needed to know how the story ended, you know? I wanted to make sure I had made the right choice." She sipped her drink. "I have to get back. Brad is about to end the set."

Hope watched Wanda return to the stage.

"She's not you," Hope told Cori. "Remember that. She's not you."

Cori was quiet on the ride back to the house. Hope didn't pose any questions. She knew that her daughter needed time to process all she had learned.

Wanda was a success, but she was not the kind of success Cori wanted. Cori had dreams. Wanda had children.

The house was dark, which was unusual. Normally, Max would have left some lights on. What was he doing?

8

Max appeared as soon as Hope flipped on the kitchen light.

"I am so sorry," Max said. "I was engrossed in an editing gig. I lost all track of time, and I must tell you that my employer is some kind of torturer. She demands that I highlight every change I make, no matter how trivial, and believe me, there are a lot of changes to be made. If I possessed the patience of Job, I wouldn't be in such a tizzy. Unfortunately, my good feelings wear thin. They make me forget my manners."

"No need to apologize. I wish there were some way to make your gigs more palatable."

"A burden I must bear. I'm certain that over time, I will grow accustomed to such ingrates."

"I'm glad you aren't totally repulsed by the people who hire you."

"What bothers me is that many of the gigs require face-to-face meetings via the computer. Mrs. Herring, I cannot do such meetings, and I can't tell them why. You would think that good work would be enough."

"Some people like to micromanage. They never learned to trust the people they hire. You'll be fine, Max. You'll see."

"I know, and now, back to work."

Max disappeared, leaving Hope to finish the bedtime duties. She was still a bit on edge about Max doing gig work online. To her way of thinking, he was taking unnecessary risks ... if such a thing could be said of a ghost.

The next morning, Hope was walking past Virginia's classroom when she noticed the picture. She stopped and stared for a moment before she entered the room. Up close the picture was even more striking.

"Do you like it?"

Hope turned to Virginia, who stood next to her.

"What is it?" Hope asked.

"An optical illusion. My husband paints them. If

you move farther left, you'll see something you didn't see before."

Hope moved to the side, and the sailing ship became a woman's face.

"That's amazing," Hope said.

"It's Walt's hobby. He took it up several years ago. He transformed the attic into his studio. He wanted to use the garage, but my car parks there. I'm not going to leave my car to the elements."

Hope moved back and forth, enticed by the changes in the painting.

"I'm using the painting to teach imaginary numbers."

"You're that advanced?"

"Not really, but I like to give the students some concepts to wrestle with. Trying to determine the square root of a negative number can be challenging."

"I see, and like the painting, not everything is as it seems."

"Exactly. If you'd like to buy one of Walt's paintings, I'll tell him you're interested."

"I think I have a place for something like this. Let me know."

"He'll be thrilled, and he needs a thrill right now."

Hope stared, and Virginia bit her lip.

"Can I trust you not to tell anyone?" the woman asked.

"I can keep a secret, as long as it has to remain a secret."

Virginia looked over her shoulder. "Walt has cancer, prostate cancer. We think he caught it quickly enough, but we're not sure. He's now in denial and depression. You know how that is. You get bad news, and you don't feel like dancing."

"I'm so sorry. Of course, I won't tell anyone. Has he started chemo?"

"It's too early for that. His urologist will do another biopsy and maybe some exploratory surgery. You know, prostate cancer is common and oftentimes is survivable. We'll see."

"In that case, set up an appointment for me. I'd like to see Walt's portfolio."

"Perfect. I'll do it and send you a text."

Hope might have given Walt's illness more thought, but she was soon inundated with the usual student angst. Small problems always seemed to mushroom into catastrophic events. Hope reduced the size of most of the issues, which allowed her to actually teach. The text from Virginia came just before the last bell.

> Walt says to come by right after school. He'll show you some of his work.

Hope replied and smiled.

"Optical illusions? Like things that look like something else if you close one eye?" Cori asked.

Hope had never been to Virginia's house, but it wasn't a long drive.

"Something like that. The whole idea is to fool the eye and the mind."

"Cool. Are you going to buy one?"

"I might."

"Can I put it in my room?"

"I don't see why not."

"Is this a teachable moment? Do you have some other motive for putting an optical illusion in my room?"

"Most moments are teachable, and yes, I think the ability to see past the obvious is an important skill. Humans are complex by nature, although they seem simple. Motives vary from the plain to the unclear. We like to take the easiest route, which is often the wrong thing to do."

"Is this about my singing career?" Cori eyed her mother.

"You have a career now?"

"You know what I mean. I want to think that you are all right with the lessons and everything."

"I'm fine with it."

"Don't worry, Mom, I'm not going to lose my head over this. I have you and Max to ground me. Dreaming never puts money in your pocket, does it?"

"Dreams are good, but they also require hard work. No one ever got famous by playing the air guitar."

Cori laughed.

Walt answered the door and while he was pale, he didn't look ill.

"Hey, hi, come in, come in. Ginny called and said you were coming. Can I get you something to drink?"

"No, no, we know you're busy," Hope said.

"Never too busy to show off my work. Although, I have to warn you that my paintings aren't what you're used to. They're all meant to change as you move around."

He led the way through the family room which showed a precision Hope could admire. She supposed Virginia's mathematical leanings contributed to the symmetry of the room. Nothing looked out of place. She and Cori followed Walt up the stairs and down the hall to the narrow door that led to the attic.

"Forgive the mess," Walt said. "I'm not a cleaner like Ginny. She complains, and I tell her artists don't have time for cleaning."

"Not to worry," Hope said. "Cori and I have our own aversions to neatness."

The attic was considerably brighter than Hope had anticipated. Two skylights helped with illumination, and they were needed because there were no windows. Around the large room were paintings ... some on display, some in stacks. Two easels stood in the middle, and both were covered with a cloth.

"I'm superstitious," he said to explain. "I don't let anyone see the work until it's finished."

"Why is that?" Cori asked.

"There are writers who won't read books while they write. They feel that the thoughts and rhythms of someone else will leak into the writer's own efforts. I'm the same way with my paintings. I show it to someone who might ask a question or offer a thought, and that non-original thought appears on the canvas. Better for me not to show them until they're finished."

"Musicians can be like that, too," Cori said. "I've

been reading. A lot of composers hide their scores until they're ready to be played."

"Exactly. So, feel free to look around. If something catches your eye, keep looking for a few seconds. It might change, as if by magic." Walt headed for the door. "I'll be back in a few minutes. Browsing is best when the artist is absent."

Walt tromped down the wooden steps, leaving Hope and Cori to roam through the attic. Hope didn't try to influence Cori, who started on the displayed canvases.

"I like the birds," Cori said. "Only they're not always birds. They turn into clouds or faces."

"That takes some skill, doesn't it? I like the ships. It seems ships with sails can be transformed into any number of things."

Like Cori, Hope was fascinated by the variety of paintings. Some were set at night, some by day. Oceans and glades mingled with deserts and clouds. She was amazed by the way the eye was led to the illusion. The waterfall drew her vision down the painting to reveal that it wasn't water at all. Clever.

"A metaphor for life," Hope said. "What you see is sometimes absolutely wrong."

"It's fun to discover things," Cori said. "Why is it

like that? Why are we amused by figuring out what isn't there?"

"Curiosity. We all like to know the truth."

A few minutes later, Walt returned. To Hope, he seemed a bit winded by the climb to the attic. That reminded her that he wasn't fully well. No doubt he wasn't as spry as he once was.

"What do you think?" Walt asked. "Find anything that you can't leave without?"

"I like the ducks," Cori said. "I think they're mallards."

"They are, and you have a good eye," Walt said. "It's new and one of my favorites."

"How much is it?" Hope asked.

"The price is dear, I'm afraid," Walt said. "It will cost you wall space."

"Wall space?" Cori asked.

"Yes, you can have the painting, if you agree to hang it on a wall where you can see it every day. I like to think my paintings will stand the test of time. I like to think that you will find them fascinating every time you look at them. So, you may take the painting with you if you'll hang it."

"Sold," Cori said. "I have just the place."

"No, we can't take it without paying something," Hope said. "That's not fair."

"Of course it's fair. My work will be advertised in your house. I'm sure people will ask about it, and you will steer them to me. Have any idea how much a billboard costs? I'm making out like a bandit."

"I don't feel good about this."

"Okay, I'll tell you what I'll do. Cori can take the mallards, and you can take this." He pulled out a painting of sailing ships that emerged from a barn. "With the same stipulation. You must hang it where visitors will see it."

"Walt, that's just more of the same."

"It is. I get twice the exposure. Come on, Hope, do me a favor. Take a look around. It's not like my stuff is selling like hotcakes, and if you really want to help me, take a photo of the painting and send it to your friends. If they say they like the work, give them my number."

Hope rolled her eyes. "All right. We'll take the paintings, and we'll hang them."

"Yay," Cori said. "Want me to send out a photo to all my buds?"

"Of course," he said. "The more, the better."

Cori took a photo of the mallards before they left the room. In the car, Hope could see that Cori was true to her word. She was sending the picture to everyone on her contacts list.

"You can't tell them what you paid," Hope said.

"I'm not going to, Mom. I'll just say it was something we could afford."

"Smart girl."

"He's just like me."

"What do you mean?"

"Mr. Zalar is just like me. He's an artist who does really good work, but no one knows. He's like me. He's waiting for someone to discover his stuff."

"With any luck, both of you will become successes. Remember his attic. It's stuffed with his paintings. He's been working hard for a long time."

"You don't have to lecture me. I can see that. How many auditions do you think I'll have to do before someone gives me a job?"

"Too many. You're going to fail far more often than you succeed. What you can't have is thin skin. You can look at it like a salesman."

"Salesman?"

"I once talked to a furniture salesman who was pushing some tables. They were nice tables, but they weren't what I was looking for. He thanked me for saying 'no.'"

"He thanked you? Why?"

"Yes, he did. He had kept track of yeses, no's, and maybes. He loved yeses. No's were just fine. He hated maybes. A 'no' was much better than a maybe because by his numbers he had one yes for every four no's. A no set him up for a sale. Three more and he'd make money."

Cori shook her head. "That's weird."

"It's the way of the world. If you play basketball and hit half your shots, then you miss the other half. A miss gets you closer to a make."

"Still weird."

Hope laughed.

Inside the house, Hope propped the painting against a wall in the family room.

"What kind of devilment is this?" Max asked.

9

Hope turned to Max who stared at the painting. "It's an optical illusion, Max. It's supposed to look like devilment."

"We had these in my day, but they were mostly confined to museums. I never saw one in a living room."

"Well, you'll be looking at this one now. The price of the painting was a promise to hang it where people would see it."

"I have one, too," Cori said and held up her painting. "It will be in my room, and you're welcome to view it whenever you want ... as long as you knock first."

"I am ever the gentleman, Cori. I believe you know that."

"Just making sure, Max."

"In time, the painting will become just another thing in the room," Hope said. "It will be as natural as sunlight."

Bijou walked in and gave the painting a curious stare.

"I do believe you. We become accustomed to our surroundings. After a short period, I will not be bedeviled."

Hope supervised as Cori hung the painting on her bedroom wall.

"This won't give me nightmares, will it?" Cori asked.

"Not unless you have something against mallards. Think of it as something that teaches you something. Sometimes things are not what they look like."

"I already know that." Cori set down the hammer.

"You do, but the painting will be a reminder. That life that looks all glitzy now might not look so glitzy if you delve into it. People love to be noticed. Sometimes, that's enough."

Cori stepped back and examined her painting. "Looks good. How about yours?"

"Not yet," Hope said. "I want to have some time to pick out the right spot."

"That Chinese thing where the room has to have the right feeling?"

"Feng Shui? I'm not a practitioner, but I do believe that where you put things does affect you. Don't ask me about ancient powers or magic or anything. Some configurations look more pleasing than others."

"Why is it that messes never seem to look right?"

Hope laughed. "A mess by definition has to look un-right."

"Un-right is not a word."

"It should be. In any case, if the scene looked pleasing, it wouldn't be called a 'mess.'"

"All right, I have to do homework."

"And I have to cook dinner. Don't let the mallards distract you too much."

"I can't wait to show it to Lottie. She'll panic."

"Panic?"

"Latest word for going ga-ga."

"Got it."

As Hope passed through the family room, she paused to study the painting. Something about it wasn't quite right, but she couldn't figure out what. She stared. No, everything seemed perfect. Why did she think otherwise? A ship under sail was a ship under sail. Shaking her head, she traipsed into the kitchen.

Before bed, Hope visited Max at his computer. He looked harried despite the khaki pants, blue shirt, and argyle vest.

"Bad day, Max?"

"When did they do away with dictionaries?"

"They didn't. They're all there online. Every word processing app has one. A thesaurus, too."

"Exactly, but the meanings of words are not the meanings I learned. I feel much more at home with a thick tome filled with pages of black-and-white definitions. I pulled up one word online, and some little imp appeared and started explaining what the word meant. I thought I knew. No, I *did* know. The imp was the one who didn't know."

"I don't want to break your heart, Max, but dictionaries are not rule books."

"What?"

"Dictionaries are histories. They tell us how words are commonly used. They don't forbid other uses. If a word acquires a new meaning, and that meaning takes root, it's added to the dictionary."

"I see. If you need a word for a particular thing, you can use one already known or make up one?"

"That's how it works."

"I shall remember. Thank you for the lesson. I believe I shall be less perturbed now."

"Indeed. How is the gig work going?"

"I am becoming better at meeting my deadlines, although I was always good at that back in the day, and so far, my work has been acceptable. No one has refused to pay."

"Excellent. Soon, you'll have a cadre of customers who depend on your abilities."

"Hah," the ghost laughed. "That will be the day. However, I do appreciate your kind words."

The next morning, Hope ran into Brad in the hallway.

"How is my favorite student?" he asked.

"Cori's fine. She practices every day."

"Great. Tomorrow is lesson day. You'll bring her?"

"I will."

"Good, but come today, after school."

"Why?"

"I have a keyboard I want Cori to learn to use."

"You don't have to do that."

"It's not a gift, Hope. It's an investment. When she goes platinum, she'll remember her old teacher and throw me a bone or something."

"I can afford a keyboard, Brad. We're not destitute."

"I know you can, but I have this one lying around gathering dust. Don't tell me Cori doesn't need something like this. The sooner we get her playing the piano, the better."

Hope thought a moment. "All right, we'll take it, but we're going to pay more for the lessons."

"We'll work that out. Stop by. I'll help load."

"Will do."

Hope wasn't entirely pleased with the gift. She didn't want Cori to think that people were going to support her without being paid. That wasn't how the world worked. Free stuff generally came with obligations attached.

At lunch, Hope ran into Virginia, her blond hair pulled into a ponytail and her brown eyes gleaming.

"Hey," Virginia said. "Walt said he gave you a couple of pictures. How do you like them?"

"We like them just fine. I'm not so sure about visitors." Hope smiled. "They might find the optical illusion disconcerting."

"Don't I know it. That's why I've limited where Walt can hang his weirdness. Try hosting a Mahjong party with those pictures all over. People can't take their eyes off them."

"They are a distraction. Make sure you tell him that we hung them where people will notice."

"That's the big deal with him. He thinks that if people see his work, he'll become famous."

"You never know."

"I know. Walt has been chasing that fantasy for years. He doesn't stand a chance. Oh well, there are worse hobbies, I guess. See you later."

Hope watched Virginia slide past Rob Flower, a PE teacher with a buzz cut and rippling muscles. As she did, she punched him lightly on the arm. He pretended that it hurt. They both laughed. The exchange made Hope wonder how well Virginia knew Rob. Well enough, it seemed.

Cori fairly bubbled in the car when Hope said they were going to pick up a keyboard. The enthusiasm made Hope smile. The keyboard was Christmas all over again. It was the unexpected gift that was exactly what Cori wanted. Santa Claus had come to the rescue.

"Here's the deal," Hope said. "The keyboard comes with a catch. You have to learn how to play it, and you have to practice."

"I will."

"I know you say that, but I'm serious. This isn't some toy you can lay aside when you're bored with it. It's a device that will make you better. It will push you toward your goal, but only if you use it."

"I know, Mom, I know."

Hope nodded, but she was pretty sure Cori didn't know. People simply couldn't fathom just how much work went into developing a talent that people would be willing to pay for. That was the true test. Was anyone willing to part with good money to listen to Cori sing? School concerts were free because people wouldn't fork over dollars to listen. What would someone pay? The biggest question of all.

Brad opened the door and grinned. "You two are the best. I can always depend upon you showing up. Come in."

The keyboard was in the basement. Hope could see that Brad had gone to the trouble to clean it and make it presentable.

"It's older, but it still works. It doesn't have the bells and whistles of modern boards, but it can make you believe you're playing a piano. That's the important part, the sound."

Hope helped Brad with the board while Cori followed with the stand, which had been folded down. The board wasn't heavy, but taking it upstairs and around corners was easier with two people. In minutes, they had it safely in the SUV.

"Can you manage it when you get home?" Brad asked. "I'd come and help, but I have an appointment."

"Not a problem," Hope asked. "Cori and I will do just fine."

Hope was true to her word. She and Cori did manage just fine, putting the keyboard in the guest bedroom. As soon as they plugged it in, Cori unfolded a chair and started to play. It wasn't a real song. It was just plinking on the keys.

"Homework first," Hope said, "then dinner and then this, got it?"

"Roger that."

Cori stood and wrapped her arms around Hope, who hugged her back.

"You're the best, Mom."

"Remember to thank Mr. Edie tomorrow when you go for your lesson. He's the one that is investing in you."

"I will, I promise."

Max turned from the computer as Hope entered the attic office.

"Was that a piano I heard?" Max asked.

"An electronic keyboard that sounds like a piano," Hope answered. "Her instructor gave it to her. It was an extra. So, now she can play while she sings."

"Fantastic. I wonder, and I know this is asking a great deal, but do you think she would let me play on the keyboard when she isn't using it?"

"I'm certain that wouldn't be a problem, but I must ask you to keep it on the quiet side when we're gone. You know why."

"I do indeed, and I shall be discreet, as ever. I can hardly wait. For the moment, I am stuck with this horrible manuscript, but soon, I will have a free hour or so. The keyboard will delight me."

Hope smiled at the ghost. "Then, we all win."

During dinner, Hope heard Max on the keyboard and Cori grinned.

"Max is going to be a lounge singer," Cori said.

Hope laughed. "I doubt they have lounge singers on the other side, but if they do, he'll be a good one."

"I'm so excited, Mom. I really am. This is happening so fast."

"It will slow down. It's like a rollercoaster ride. Sometimes fast and sometimes slow."

"After dinner, I'll practice."

After Cori had gone to bed, Hope stopped in the guest room. She touched the keyboard and wondered if it held the magic Cori wanted. Time would tell. She asked herself if she had what it would take to keep up with Cori. Hope would have to consider that. Would Cori do better with a manager?

Hope shook her head. She was way ahead of the curve. At the moment, her daughter had a school music teacher for a coach and a very used keyboard. To envision that into a career was silly.

The next day flew past. Hope looked for Brad in the halls and lounge, but he wasn't around. Not that it mattered. If he had a change of plans, he would text.

In the SUV, Cori tapped her foot fast.

"You're like Thumper the rabbit," Hope told her.

"I can't help it," Cori said. "I want to show him how much I've learned."

"Soon enough. Just relax. I'm sure he'll tell you that. You'll sing better if you just let the voice come."

"Yeah, yeah."

Brad's house looked dark, but that didn't mean anything.

"You know what to do," Hope said. "If you're going to run a little long, text me. Otherwise, I'll be back in an hour."

Hope watched until Cori was inside the house,

then Hope backed out of the driveway and started away. She hadn't gone a block before her phone pinged.

Cori.

Hope opened the one-word text.

> HELP!!!!

10

Cori stood in the open the door as Hope approached, and one look at her daughter told her that Cori was half in shock. The teen pointed into the house.

"He's just inside," Cori whispered.

"911?" Hope asked.

"I'll do it," Cori answered, taking her phone from her back pocket.

Hope stepped into the main room and stopped.

On the floor ahead of her was Brad's body. His chest was a bloody mess, and it was pretty easy to see that he was dead. Still, Hope knew enough to do due diligence. She knelt down beside him and felt for a pulse. His skin was cold, lips blue, and face white.

Nothing.

Brad had been dead for a while. She had no idea how long, and she wasn't going to guess. She stood and stepped out of the room. She found Cori at the front door, still on her phone. Hope held out her hand.

"He's dead," Hope said. "I just checked for a pulse. There's no hurry on the ambulance. I haven't searched the house for an intruder, but I doubt there's anyone here. The body is cold. We'll meet the police outside the house."

Hope shooed Cori out but not before Cori fetched her backpack.

"Before things get harried and complicated, walk me through what happened."

"Nothing happened," Cori said. "I opened the door, walked in, and then I found ... him. That was when I texted you."

"Did you touch anything? Did you notice anything out of sorts?"

Cori shook her head. "I don't remember touching anything. I ... I didn't try to see if he was alive. Should I have?"

"He looked very dead, Cori. You did the right thing. When the police question you, tell them the truth. That's all you can do."

"I will."

A police cruiser pulled to the curb and two uniformed policemen stepped out. One of them stayed with Hope and Cori, while the other went inside.

"Who found the body?" the policeman asked.

"I did," Cori said. "He's my voice teacher, and I came for a lesson."

"He was already dead?"

"I think so. I didn't check. He looked dead."

"I checked," Hope said. "I didn't find a pulse."

The other police officer stepped out. "Gunshot wound to the chest. Call it in. I'll check the rest of the house."

The police officer returned to the house.

"Do you two mind standing by the car?" the other police officer asked. "It's going to get busy here in a few minutes."

"I'll move my car," Hope offered.

"That might help."

The ambulance arrived before the forensic team, and the techs arrived before the coroner. Last to show up was Detective Robinson, an African American law enforcement officer whom Hope had worked with for several years. He stopped by to talk to Hope and Cori before he went into the house.

"What can you tell me?" the handsome man asked.

"Cori had a lesson planned with Brad, the victim. He's ... he was her voice coach. I dropped her off. She went inside, found the body, and texted me. I hadn't gone a mile. I came back, saw that Brad was indeed dead, and Cori called 911. I touched the body to make sure he wasn't alive. Cori can tell you what she touched."

"Nothing," Cori said. "I ... I freaked. I didn't know what to do except call Mom."

"Understandable. I'm going in now. Please, if you will, wait for me out here."

Hope nodded. "We'll be here."

"I don't want to wait for him," Cori said as soon as the detective was our of earshot. "I want to go home." The teen's face was pale.

"I don't either," Hope said, "but we found the body. We're on the hook."

"We're suspects?"

"In a word, yes."

"But, he was shot a long time ago. That has to mean we're innocent."

"A clever killer might well commit the crime, leave for a few hours, and then come back for the discovery. I mean, especially with a gunshot wound, the killer might go home and shower and remove any trace of gunpowder. The shooter will look innocent."

"The killer would have to have an awful lot of confidence to do that."

"He would, and the killer would still need an alibi, but it is clever."

"You're that clever, aren't you?"

"No, Cori, I'm not, not when crime is concerned. No matter how clever you are, there are a hundred different details that you would need to cover. You'd be lucky to think of a third of them. People always wonder why criminals make stupid mistakes. It's because they can't think of everything. It's impossible."

Detective Robinson came out of the house and approached Cori and Hope.

"I don't want to keep you," the detective said. "Will you be available for questioning tomorrow or the next day?"

"We will," Hope said. "Though it would be helpful if you could make it after school."

"Sure, sure. Look, Hope, I don't have a handle on this one yet. Since nothing seems to be missing, and the house wasn't ransacked, it looks as if the victim knew the shooter."

"I thought the same thing."

"He taught at the school?"

"Yes, music, and he coached the band and choral group."

"Okay, makes sense. Be careful going home. Oh, Cori, if you need to talk to someone other than your mother, there are resources available. Let me know and I can set you up with someone."

"Thank you," Cori said. "I'll think about it."

On the way home, Cori was quiet, and she wasn't using her phone either, which was unusual.

"Want to talk about it?" Hope asked.

"Omens," Cori replied.

"The movies?"

"What if his death is some kind of omen? What if I'm not meant to be a singer?"

"Omens imply fate, and I don't think we can put much stock in fate. I don't think you have a preordained destiny. Neither do I. We live our lives one day at a time. From waking to sleeping. That's about it. While we think we have some control over our lives, that's not always true."

"I don't know, Mom. Some kids at school think they're doomed. No matter what they do, they're not going to make it."

"Teenagers, by definition, are a moody and

pessimistic lot. It comes with the realization that sooner or later they have to join the real world. They have to work, make and keep friends, maybe have a family, make mistakes, and fight ... yes, fight. No one is going to give them all that they want. They have to work for what's important to them, and they're not at all sure they're up to it."

"I know all that. You've prepped me pretty well for that. But, I no sooner get a voice coach than he dies. No, he was murdered. It's as if someone is trying to tell me something."

"Brad was a good person. He was kind and helpful, and we'll both miss him. What happened to him doesn't have anything to do with your singing. This is out of your control. Someone killed him. When they find out who, they'll arrest, try, and sentence the killer, provided the jury agrees. There are no angels sitting in the heavens that decided the death or the outcome."

"I know, I know, but ... it feels so hard now."

"I know it does. It's been a terrible shock, but you can't let what happened to him turn you away from your interest in singing. The death isn't a sign, and it's not an omen. If you let things knock you off your path, there might not be someone out there to help nudge you back on to it. I heard a speaker once counsel that you never tell people your problems. Eighty percent of those people don't care, and the other twenty percent are glad you have problems."

Cori chuckled. "That's good advice, I guess."

"Yes, it's funny because it's mostly true. Hopefully, you'll always have someone who will want to listen to you when you're sad and happy, but there are always a lot of people who will try to discourage you from doing things. They'll say they want you to succeed, but they really don't. That's human nature sometimes. Judge your friends by what they do, not what they say."

"I already do that."

Hope could tell that her little talk in the car hadn't done much for Cori. A silent tear ran down her daughter's cheek, and she wiped it away.

"Ice cream," Hope said. "Ice cream sometimes does some good. I think we have a box of Neapolitan in the freezer."

"Yeah."

At home in the kitchen, Hope placed a bowl of ice cream in front of Cori, and Max appeared. He resembled a WWI pilot with boots, jodhpurs, a shirt, a leather jacket, a silk scarf, a helmet, and goggles.

"Going after the Red Baron?" Hope asked.

"Ice cream before dinner?" he answered.

"Cori wasn't able to take her lesson today," Hope told the ghost. "Her voice coach has been murdered."

"Gads, that's horrible. I trust the murderer is in custody?"

"No, Max, he's in the wild. There will be some work to be done before he stands before a judge."

"No direct threat to us?"

"Not that we can see. It was unfortunate that Cori found the body, but that's what happened."

"It's not a holiday," Cori said, "which makes it none of our business." The teen believed that on every holiday, her mother would be called in by Detective Robinson to work on a case with him because on nearly every holiday for the past couple of years, that was what had happened.

Max chuckled. "Correct. You and your mother work only on those murders that happen around holidays."

"I think we debunked that theory," Hope said. "And, I don't think we'll be involved in this case. I don't see a reason to be unless the police think otherwise."

"Since Cori found the victim, I doubt they would ask for your services, Mrs. Herring."

"Good," Cori said. "I just want the police to find

the killer. We'll all be better off for that." She patted Bijou who had jumped onto her lap.

"I believe a second helping of ice cream is in order," Max said. "You can never eat too much ice cream. Well, most of the time."

Hope waited all evening for a call from Detective Robinson. She was ready to set a time for an interview. Instead, she found herself in bed, staring at the ceiling. She couldn't help but wonder who had killed Brad and for what reason. As far as she knew, he had no enemies. Then again, she didn't know much about him. He was gay. She knew that, and he had a significant other who didn't live in Castle Park. Love triangles were as old as dirt. Revenge was a third. Who had killed him and why?

She chided herself. She was acting like she was going to work the case when she wasn't. She didn't need to know the motive. She didn't want to know the motive. Someone had shot Brad, and that someone would pay. Why that someone had fired the shot was not her concern. She rolled over and closed her eyes. She was going to sleep.

Detective Robinson sent her a text the next day. He would come to her classroom after school. If Hope and Cori could both be there, that would be just fine. He didn't think a visit to the police station was necessary. Hope was happy about that.

Cori arrived first, and Hope could see that she was nervous. The dark circles under her daughter's eyes said she hadn't slept well the previous night.

"No need to be scared," Hope said. "You didn't do anything wrong. So, we go from there."

"You'll stay with me?"

"I sure will."

"Why did he die?"

Hope was surprised by the question. After all, Cori had lost her father before they moved to North Carolina. She had seen death several times since Hope started solving mysteries.

"He didn't choose to die," Hope said. "We don't yet know why he was killed. Motive is a difficult thing to prove. Even if the murderer confesses, you can't know if it's the truth. All we do know is that someone wanted Brad dead. Reasons are as old as humanity."

"There is no real order to the universe, is there?"

"If there is a grand plan, I don't know about it. No one does, but that's sort of the goal. If you already know the plan, where's the joy in doing anything?"

"Huh?"

"If you know the merry-go-round of your life,

why live it? That's boredom. It's the unknowable that keeps us going. It's the surprises, both good and bad. I hope that makes sense."

"Maybe. Where am I going to find another voice coach?"

"We'll find someone for you to work with."

"In the grand plan, do you think I wasn't supposed to work with Mr. Edie?"

"I have no idea. We muddle through, remember?"

Cori nodded. "We do."

Detective Robinson entered Hope's classroom, and he wasn't smiling.

"All right, I don't have a lot of time. Who wants to go first?"

11

"That would be me," Cori answered.

"Have a seat. Start when you're ready. Just tell me what you did."

Cori sat and went through the arrival at Brad's house and her discovery of the corpse.

"No one else was there?"

Cori shook her head.

"No mess, no sign of robbery?"

"No, sir. Everything looked all right to me."

"Good. So, you called your mother. Then what?"

"It was only a few minutes before Mom came. She checked for a pulse. I called 911."

"Again, you didn't notice anything amiss?"

"No, sir. I was too upset, and anyway, I've only been in Mr. Edie's house a couple of times."

"Then what happened?"

"We waited outside for the police to come."

The detective nodded and turned to Hope. "Anything to add?"

"Not really. When I didn't find any sign of life, I thought it best to wait outside. We'd already contaminated the murder scene. There was no need to do more."

"Exactly, and thank you for that. Now, do you own a firearm?"

Hope nodded. "An automatic pistol. I keep it at home."

"What caliber?"

"Nine millimeter."

"Do you mind if we test it?"

"I'll bring it to the station."

"Great. Look, I can't ask either of you to be involved in this case. As of right now, you're not suspects, but you did find the body. So, we'll start there. We believe the deceased died the night before you found him. Therefore, I have to ask you what you were doing between the hours of eight and midnight that night."

"We were home," Hope said. "We can't prove that, but it's the truth. I teach. Cori goes to school. We get up early. We don't stay out late."

"That works for me. If either of you remember something more, contact me. Thank you for your time."

Hope waited until she was certain the detective had left before she turned to Cori.

"That's over. We're off the hook."

Looking tired and worn out, Cori stood. "How do I erase the image from my brain?"

"Time. Time will blur the edges and remove the colors. It's like an old photograph. Over time, it becomes a blurry impression. Crazy, but true."

"I can't wait until that happens."

Back at home, Hope went up to her attic office and saw Max. The ghost was wearing a hip-hop outfit of sagging jeans, an oversized T-shirt, and high-top sneakers. To Hope, he was the oddest-looking rapper she had ever seen.

"I must confess that I was listening, Mrs. Herring," Max said. "It appears that you won't be involved with the case."

"I won't be, and I have to admit it feels kind of nice for a change."

"Do you want me to go online and look for a new voice coach for Cori?"

"No, Max, that's her job. We can't want a singing career for her more than she does."

"Well said and very true. I must return to my gig now. There is a lot to learn about modern music."

Hope started to consider just how Brad had died, but stopped herself. The murder was not hers to work.

Murder?

Was it murder?

Or, had Brad shot himself in the chest? That might make sense, if they had found a pistol at the scene or a note. She shook her head. She wasn't walking down that path.

After school the next day, Virginia walked into Hope's classroom. Despite heavy makeup, Hope could tell that Virginia had been crying. The woman's smile was subdued also. Those were signs that Virginia was about to share some sort of pain.

Bad news.

"Got a minute?" Virginia asked.

"Always. What's going on?"

"Is it that obvious? Oh, wait, you're a detective. Of course, you'd notice any problems."

"Have a seat." Hope gestured to a chair.

Virginia took one of the student desks facing Hope. With a little imagination, Hope could transform her into a student who needed help with a complicated topic, but she didn't want to use that much imagination.

"Have you ever felt guilty over someone's untimely death?" Virginia asked.

"No, not really. I've been involved in a few murders, but I never was the cause."

"Brad Edie. I don't know if I'm the reason he's dead."

"You'll have to explain that."

"My story is as old as the Bible. I'm married, but I found Brad ... irresistible. He is ... was so vibrant and daring. He had all the energy my marriage was missing. I know that sounds self-serving, and I suppose it is, but it's true. I became infatuated with him, even though I knew he was gay. Well, he also liked women, and I took full advantage of that."

Virginia stopped and bit her lip. Hope wondered if that was some kind of act, something to stoke her feelings. If it was, it wasn't working.

Virginia went on. "An affair between two teachers is enough to get us both canned. In my case, this wasn't some kind of long-term plan. It was being together, pure and simple. I wasn't going to leave Walter. Brad wasn't going to dump his significant other. Because of that, we were extra careful. We both knew that the other one wouldn't be there if a problem occurred."

"I'll buy that. You're telling me you have no motive for any murder."

"Yes and no. I'd developed some deep feelings for Brad. I'd approached him about it just a few weeks ago. He was kind, and he said he would think about it, but I didn't believe him. I was stunned, of course. I thought, well, I thought we had reached a point where love might bring us together. You must think me an idiot, one of those women who think they can convert a fling into something permanent. Dumb, dumb, dumb."

"People often try to change the stripes on a tiger. It doesn't often work."

Virginia sighed. "Don't I know it. I'm a grown woman. I realized that Brad was in this for the good times. I didn't blame him. I blame myself. I invested more than he did. Like I said, an old story."

"So, why are you telling me this?"

Virginia tapped her fingers on the desk; a nervous action. "Like I said, we were discreet. It was easier to hide, since Brad had a male partner. I'm not so naive as to believe that the truth won't come out now. I'm sure they'll find my fingerprints inside his house. I'm sure they'll want to question me. When that happens, Walt will be hurt, very hurt. He trusts me implicitly. I trust him. Our marriage might not survive the revelation. Not to mention that he's so sick. If the cancer doesn't kill him, my infidelity might."

"I don't see where I'm involved," Hope said.

"You ... you found the body, right?"

"Cori and I did, yes. But, we were inside for only a matter of minutes. I didn't see anything that might help you."

Virginia bit her lip. "Yeah, I was pretty sure of that. We didn't leave an online trail either. None of those gushy little messages that create a trail. I wanted to, I really did. Brad made it clear that he would not welcome such messages."

"Did you kill him?"

"No, God no, I loved him."

"Many people have murdered the people they love. It's a perverse action, but it's not unheard of."

"I wouldn't. I couldn't. Look, I knew that sooner or later he was going to move on. That was a bitter pill to swallow, but it's the truth."

"Where were you the night he died?" Hope asked.

"Home, in bed, asleep. Walt can vouch for that."

"Good. You're off the hook then."

"I know, but should I go to the police? I can wait for them to come to me. Is that wise?"

"I'm not an attorney," Hope said. "I don't have any privilege. If the police ask me about this conversation, I'll have to tell them the truth."

"I ... I didn't think of that. Have I cooked my own goose?"

"No. Again, you haven't revealed anything worse than an ill-timed love affair. Luckily, people don't go to jail for that. If they did, well, I would venture that we would need more prisons."

"Amen to that."

"So, it comes down to whether revealing your affair is better than keeping it hidden. I think you might find that the police will keep it a secret as long as it's not material to the investigation. As you said, your prints are going to be there. If you left any clothes there, they might find your DNA also. They'll be able to show that you were there. They will probably want to talk to you. You don't have to go to them, but I would suggest that it's a good thing to do. You can explain what you and Brad had. You can offer Walter as your alibi. After all, what loved one wouldn't try to keep you out of jail?"

"It's all I have."

"Exactly. If you were a clever murderer, you would have a better alibi."

"But I don't have to go to the police?"

"No, you can wait. You don't have to reveal your affair, but that's a risky play. If they discover it, you'll look as if you're guilty."

"I know. Roll the dice, right? What would you do?"

"I can't tell you. You have to make your own decisions."

"I can explain away the fingerprints. After all, we're fellow teachers. It's not at all unusual for teachers to visit each other. Nothing odd about that. I'm pretty sure I didn't leave any clothes at Brad's, nothing that would be identified as mine." Virginia blushed. "There are a couple of teddies. I don't think they'll find any DNA there."

"Please, Virginia, don't think out loud. I don't want to have to admit I heard you."

"I'm sorry. I ... well, I think of you as someone who wouldn't blab all you know."

"But I won't lie."

"No, no, no, nothing like that. I'm going to walk the tightrope. I'm not going to the police. If they come to me, I'll tell them about Brad. They'll understand why I didn't come forward."

"They might. They might wonder why you didn't come forward and help them find the killer."

"That's easy. I didn't want to expose myself to my husband."

"What if he's the killer?"

Virginia blinked. "Not Walter. He doesn't have a jealous bone in his body. Don't take that the wrong way. He loves me. I'm sure of that. He just can't kill ... anything. He has trouble stepping on a spider."

"Good. You might want to go back and remember all the times you and Brad were together. Where you went, what you did."

"We never—"

Hope held up her hand. "I'm sure you were careful around here, but if you hooked up in some other city or town, well, you might not have felt the need to be discreet."

Virginia frowned. "I never thought about that."

"Every phone is a surveillance camera. Anymore, most places have cameras in place. Facial recognition software will identify you."

"True, true, but I've decided. I'm going to go mum until they contact me."

"You don't have anything that will help them catch the killer?"

"They already know. Brad's jealous boyfriend. I

wasn't the only one who needed to keep our affair quiet. Brad told me more than once that Chuck was volatile. He'd had his share of fights in bars." Virginia stood. "I'm pretty sure Chuck has a pistol, too."

"A pistol? Is that important?" Hope asked wondering how Virginia knew Brad had been shot.

Virginia's eyes widened, like a deer in the headlights. "I ... I thought Brad was shot. I mean, that's the rumor. Am I wrong?"

"No. I think you're right. I just wondered how you knew."

"The teachers' lounge. I'm sure I heard it there."

"Probably. Do you have a pistol?"

"I don't think I should answer that."

"I understand."

"I'm not trying to get away with anything, Hope. I'm trying to salvage my marriage. Maybe that's wrong. Maybe, it's impossible. Walter and I have a good life. I don't want that to end."

Virginia walked out, leaving Hope to wonder. Virginia seemed to have more secrets that she wasn't sharing. What were they?

Hope shook her head. No, she wasn't getting involved. She was sitting this one out. Detective

Robinson was more than smart enough to find Virginia and question her.

On the drive home, Cori gave Hope the news. "I've contacted three voice coaches. I found them online, and I plan to interview them. Want to help?"

12

"Sure," Hope said. "Although, I'm pretty sure I'll vote for the closest one."

"That's fair, I guess. They all have good ratings. I suppose it comes down to finding one I feel comfortable with."

"Online interviews?"

"To start with, yeah, until I'm ready to meet them in person. This isn't too big of a pain in the neck, is it?"

"No, Cori, not yet. It's a matter of money and schedule. You still have school and all that entails."

"I won't neglect my studies. I am so sorry Mr. Edie is gone."

"Me too."

"Do they know who killed him?"

"Not yet."

"They'll figure it out, even without you."

"Without us. You've always worked these cases with me."

Cori looked out the window a moment, which caused Hope to glance over. "What are you thinking?"

"When will it stop?" Cori asked.

"When will what stop?"

"The murders. When will the murders stop?"

"Murders will never stop, Cori. That's the nature of humans. People kill each other. That's as old as the Garden of Eden ... Cain and Abel. The reasons vary. Sometimes, it's war. Sometimes, it's money. Sometimes, it's jealousy or envy or some other emotion. Humans don't need a lot of prodding. They kill and murder on a regular basis. I don't think that will stop as long as humans are ... human. I wish I had a different answer for you, but that's the way of our world."

"But, when will we stop getting involved?"

"I don't know. That's the honest truth. It's not like we're involved in every murder around here. You're right, though. We've been involved in far too many. Most people go through life without being involved in a single murder investigation. We, well, we haven't been so lucky. The murders are bound to end for us. It's just a matter of time."

"Yeah."

At home, Hope found Max in the attic office. He wore a beret, a striped top, jeans, and boots. Hope couldn't quite figure out if he was trying to be a mime or something else.

"What are you today, Max?"

"I am rewriting a screenplay, and I wanted to feel like a director. Does the outfit work?"

"I suppose so, although you might need a silk scarf to keep your neck warm."

"Do you have any experience with writing screenplays? It is decidedly different than writing novels or stories. The conventions are rather daunting. I had no idea what a slug line was before today, and dialogue baffles me. How is one to pass along vital information and still make the dialogue sound real?"

"That's why they pay screenwriters big bucks. How did you manage to land a screenplay gig?"

"I was the low bidder, I believe. I mean, I looked up some scripts online, and they did not appear to be all that difficult to write. Most of the page is blank, and the descriptions are sparse at best. I thought it would be a snap. However, it is proving difficult to give each character a distinct voice. Does that sound correct?"

"It does, but then, I'm no screenwriter. I can barely turn out a passable paragraph."

"Balderdash, Mrs. Herring. You are an accomplished teacher. I know you can produce lucid prose on demand."

"Thank you for the vote of confidence, but I'll be of no help to you. I know nothing about screenplays. I'm afraid you're on your own, Max."

He frowned. "I was hoping... Oh, well, I will wade through this and get it finished. I might not get paid a bonus. I might not get paid at all. Yet, I shall persevere." He touched his beret.

Hope was halfway through making dinner when the doorbell rang. She was pretty certain Cori was in her room, probably with earbuds in place, and Max couldn't answer. Shrugging, Hope walked down the hall with Bijou ahead of her, opened the door, and found Walter Zalar on the porch.

"Walter," Hope said. "Come in, come in."

"I won't take much of your time," Walter said as he passed by her. "I hope you're not busy."

Bijou stared at the man, her tail flicking back and forth.

"I'm making dinner." Hope closed the door. "Follow me."

Hope led the older man into the kitchen. She noticed he walked with a decided limp.

"Something happen to your leg, Walter?"

"I fell off a ladder. Not a long fall; I just landed oddly."

"I'm sorry to hear that. You went to the emergency room?"

"No, no, it wasn't that bad. Besides, Virginia didn't mean to bump the ladder. No need to explain that."

"She bumped the ladder?"

"She was in a hurry. She had someplace to be. You know how it goes. I was adjusting a cabinet door. She ran past. It was really my fault. I'm not as balanced as I once was."

"Does your treatment have something to do with your balance issues?"

"Treatment?"

"Virginia told me you're having treatment for cancer."

"Cancer?" He laughed. "Virginia told you that? I don't have cancer. I admit that I'm not as spry as I once was, but that's not due to any disease."

"But, Virginia ... well, I suppose I misunderstood."

"Most probably."

"I'm sorry about the confusion. Can I get you something?"

"Got a beer?"

"I believe I do. Light beer okay?"

"Sure, beer is beer."

Hope fetched a beer from the fridge as the man settled at the table with a sigh.

"Don't get old, Hope. Everything hurts."

She slid onto a chair. "I'm afraid growing older can't be avoided."

"Maybe they'll have better drugs by the time you get to my age."

"You're not that old, Walt. What brings you by?"

"Brad Edie."

"Brad? What about Brad?" Hope was more than a little surprised, especially after Virginia's confession.

"You knew Brad pretty well, right? I mean, I heard he was tutoring your daughter."

"He had given her exactly one lesson, so he wasn't exactly tutoring."

"Doesn't matter, doesn't matter. Here's my dilemma. I keep the books for most of the clubs at the high school. That includes the band. Brad always decided things, but he's gone. So, I was wondering if it would be appropriate for the band to send flowers. You know, to the funeral parlor."

"I don't know. I mean, the clubs probably have bylaws, right?"

"Special circumstances. I think his death would fall under that paragraph."

"What did Virginia say?"

Walt rubbed his chin as if trying to think. "I didn't run it past her. I suppose you probably know, but Virginia had a run in with Brad not long ago."

"I didn't know."

"Yeah, it was about a girl in the high school. Rumor was that Brad and her ... well, I told Virginia that Brad was gay. He wasn't going to mess with some teenager."

"That makes sense. You say Virginia knew about Brad and the girl?"

"No, no, I can't say she knew for sure. It was a rumor, you know? You won't tattle on me, will you?"

"I don't pass along rumors, Walt."

"Good, great, so what do you think, the principal?"

"I would start there, and I think it would be a

great gesture. No one is going to say no to sending some flowers."

"You're right. I'll talk to the principal and then I'll make arrangements." He stood. "Thanks for the beer."

"I'll see you out."

As Hope closed the door, she couldn't help but wonder about Virginia. Why didn't Walt's story mesh with Virginia's? Hope stood at the stove and considered things for a moment. Walt certainly didn't have a clue as to what Virginia was doing with Brad. She felt sorry for him. She thought he deserved better.

No, no, Hope was not going to think about Brad, Virginia, or Walter. She wasn't involved in it. She would go to the funeral. She would see Brad buried. Then, she would forget. She would focus on her daughter. It was that simple and that final.

"We have an appointment tomorrow," Cori said between bites of stir fry, "in Burgaw."

"That's doable," Hope said. "What should I know?"

"Norrie Patrick sang on Broadway for years and years. She's old. I looked her up online. She was in some of the most successful musicals of all time."

"I see. The lead?"

"Yep. Not opera, but singing on stage. I think that makes her qualified."

"Any of her students make it?"

"Yes, several have had hits. They've been on TV and in concerts."

"Any names I would recognize?"

"No, I don't think so."

"Doesn't matter. How did she sound on the phone?"

"We texted. She has an opening."

"I tend to think that they will all have an opening. Expensive?"

"Cheaper than Mr. Edie, really."

"Sounds like Ms. Patrick could be a contender."

"I agree. So, the appointment is on?"

"You made it. I'll take you there."

"I saw Mr. Zalar leave. Can you tell me what he wanted?"

"He wanted to know if he should send flowers to Mr. Edie's funeral."

"He had to ask you about that?" Cori looked puzzled.

"He was sending them from the band, using band money."

"Oh, yeah, I understand. He can't just do it, can he?"

"He's going to the principal, where he should have gone anyway."

"Why was he limping?"

"He fell off a ladder."

"Roger that."

Max appeared, wearing his director's clothes, and he took a seat at the table.

"Excuse me," Max said, "but I've just spent an hour with the most demanding person I've ever met. Nothing but inane notes about story elements I know nothing about. Have you heard of 'Save the Cat'? Neither did I until this person brought it up. I'm supposed to come up with a scene that shows the hero saving a cat ... metaphorically speaking. It demonstrates how nice he is deep down. No matter what sort of havoc he creates in the story, he's really a nice guy."

"Sounds right to me," Cori said.

"Of course, it sounds nice. How am I to invent such a scene? I can't very well have him saving a dog or something. Oh, I guess I could, but that doesn't mean it will fit into the story or theme. Oh, theme, now there's a concept my tormenter doesn't understand. A genre is not a theme. I know that much."

"You have your hands full," Hope said. "I hope the money is worth it."

"That's just it. The sum is paltry. I was better off editing that tome about conspiracy theories. Did you know that some people believe that aliens from space have landed, been captured, and are now living in Utah? They're pretending to be Mormons."

Hope laughed, as did Cori.

"It's true. According to the book I battled, they are hiding until their mother ship returns. Then, they will decide whether to leave or simply destroy the planet."

"That client has seen too many Star Wars movies," Cori said. "Destroying a planet isn't something that can be done."

"Who knows?" Max stretched. "I'm a ghost. I shouldn't feel so tired. Where do these people come from?"

"I'm sure your next gig will be better," Hope said.

"I don't see how it could be any worse, Mrs. Herring. I just don't."

"Things can always get worse," Hope kidded.

"Roger that," Cori said.

Max laughed.

After rinsing the dishes and loading the dishwasher, Cori disappeared into her room. Hope heard her practicing her vocal exercises, and that made her think about Brad, and Brad led to Virginia, and

Virginia led to Walter. What a weird triangle that was. Well, it wasn't a triangle anymore. Had Hope been working with the police, she would have informed Detective Robinson of the affair, but she wasn't working with the police.

Virginia had an alibi and no motive. That made all the difference in the world.

Hope pushed aside the triangle and thought about school the next day. It was time for a pop quiz. The students wouldn't be happy about that, but they had been warned about the possibility.

The next morning, Hope checked her phone while she sipped her coffee. There was a text from a name she didn't recognize. No, she *did* recognize it. Why did Brad's partner want to talk to her?

13

Norrie Patrick lived in a dated farmhouse, set in front of a dated barn. Pine trees, a staple of North Carolina forests surrounded the house and barn, separating them from fields of cotton, glimpsed between the trees. As Hope approached the long porch, she wondered if Norrie did any farming, or did she rent the land to some other farmer. Not that it mattered. Cori led the way, and Cori knocked on the door. Hope was perfectly at ease, letting Cori take over.

To Hope, Norrie Patrick was elegant. With lovely white hair, a slender body, and a back still straight, she was the epitome of an actress. The woman had a presence that Hope had rarely seen. More, she did it effortlessly, as if born to command attention. Hope noticed that Cori was impressed as well.

"You must be the Herrings," Norrie said. Her voice was quiet, yet powerful. Hope guessed years on the stage had strengthened Norrie's vocal cords.

"We are," Cori answered. "I'm Cori, and this is my mom, Hope."

Norrie shook hands. "I'm very glad to meet you. Won't you come in?"

A huge room occupied the front of the house. The walls were covered with photos—of Norrie. They showed her in the various roles she had played on stage and in movies. They showed no real age progression, although Hope thought she could find one if she worked hard enough. The photos highlighted a career that had spanned decades.

"Do you like them?" Norrie asked.

"They are quite impressive," Hope said. "I'm old enough to remember most of these shows."

"They don't write them like that anymore," Norrie said. "Come, I have lemonade and tea waiting on the patio. I would like to chat with you two for a few minutes."

Norrie led the way through a music room—piano, recording equipment, and video equipment.

Hope didn't spot any other instruments, which told her Norrie specialized in voice and ... presence. French doors led to the patio where they settled at a glass-top table under a large, pink umbrella. Norrie poured, while Hope gazed out over a green lawn and blue pool.

"This must be a blessing at dawn and dusk," Hope said.

"It is," Norrie said. "The birds come then. This year has been the year of the woodpecker. The trees are full of redheaded woodpeckers, who keep up a steady drumbeat."

"We don't have so many in town," Hope said. "I suppose there are too many humans and houses around."

"Since I moved here, I've discovered the food chain."

"Food chain?" asked Cori. "What do you mean?"

"When I arrived, this house and barn were home to a great many snakes, far more than I was comfortable with. At night, snakes like to hide in the deep shadows. I was on the phone complaining to one of my friends, when he informed me that I had snakes because I had creatures that snakes ate. I was flabbergasted. I hadn't thought of it in those terms. I did some research and started cleaning up the property. I got rid of the mice and moles and voles and small prey by making sure there was nothing for them to munch on. I have the barn and house treated on a regular basis, which eliminates the insects that frogs, toads, and lizards eat. The birds can nest in the trees, and that's where the snakes go for eggs. They avoid the house because there is no prey. So, if you wish to rid yourself of a pest, eliminate what the pest eats. Food chain."

"Cool," Cori said.

"Now, Cori, tell me why you want to become a singer, and it's all right to admit that you want fame and fortune. There is no shame in ambition. No one makes it without the drive, no matter how beautiful the voice."

"Excuse me," Hope said. "How long will the interview take?"

"I would think an hour or so," Norrie answered.

"I hate to leave, but I have an appointment with someone. Sean's Breakfast isn't far from here, is it?"

"A few minutes."

"I'll be back within an hour," Hope said. "I promise." She turned to Cori. "I'm trusting you to do what is asked."

"No worries, Mom."

Hope stood, kissed Cori's cheek, and headed out of the house. "Thank you, Ms. Patrick."

"Call me Norrie, and I'll take good care of her."

Hope berated herself for leaving her daughter, but it was the best she could do.

Sean's Breakfast occupied what Hope guessed was an old gas station. Tiny, with the kitchen in plain sight, it smelled of grease and cigars. Someone had smoked there. She hoped it was always after closing time.

All the worn, wooden tables were empty, except for one. She recognized the lone man sitting there, as a photo of him had been in Brad's house and she'd met him once at school. There was no doubt that the tanned, bald man was Chuck Newton, Brad's significant other. He stood as she approached.

"Hope?" he asked.

She nodded. "Mr. Newton?"

"Please, call me Chuck. Mr. Newton is my father. Coffee?"

"Yes." Hope offered condolences to Chuck, and the man thanked her.

Chuck waved to an older woman who lounged behind the empty counter. She nodded, which told Hope that he was a known customer.

"I have to thank you for coming," Chuck said.

"I'd like to say we have all evening to chat, but Sean's will close in a little bit. And, I have to get home. I have a deadline."

"Deadline?"

"I'm a freelance journalist. I do gigs. Right now, I'm a bit stuck. I hired someone online to edit a rather long article. So far, my editor hasn't completed the assignment. I have to track him or her down and see what the problem is."

Hope wanted to ask if the editor was named Max, but she stopped herself. She didn't want to open that can of worms.

"Good luck with that. I don't know if I would trust the net to provide a good editor."

"Yeah, well, it's not always easy to reach the person you've hired. You send emails and maybe texts, but they don't always get answered. Hey, I'm sorry. I didn't mean to burden you with my problems. I asked you here to talk about Brad."

Hope nodded. "So you did."

"Well, there's the issue of the keyboard he lent you."

"Oh, right, don't worry, I'll get that back to you."

"No, no. Brad wanted your daughter to have it, so please keep it. I'm the executor of his estate so she keeps it."

"That's very generous."

"It is. The second thing isn't about Brad, well, not directly. Brad was ... well, I loved him. I have to admit that. I don't want his murderer to get away with it."

"No one wants to see a loved one killed without someone paying."

"Exactly. Since you are the foremost murder solver in this neck of the woods, I want you to investigate."

"I can't. I'm sorry, but I can't. Because Cori and I discovered the body, we're on the suspect list. I don't have access to any evidence gathered by the police."

"That's hogwash. He was already dead. Dead for hours, right? You shouldn't be considered a suspect."

"Perhaps not, but I don't make the rules."

He frowned. "What if I make a stink of it? I mean, I have access to some media. I get some publicity, and maybe you can get to do what you do."

"Please, don't. I have a good relationship with the police. I wouldn't want them to resent me."

"I want this case solved."

"It will be. You simply have to be a little patient."

He sipped coffee. "You think I did it, don't you?"

"What? No, why would I think that? I don't know you."

"I don't blame you. I think the police will discover that Brad and I had our share of arguments. We're a couple. We're supposed to battle."

"Did you battle?"

"Once. It was after one of his ... indiscretions. That's how he referred to the times he cheated. You may think that gays don't get jealous, but we do. We're human. I have to admit that I got the better of it. I was so ... angry, but I stopped myself before I did any permanent damage. And, I never used a weapon. I'm sure that when the police investigate, they'll find out about the fight. They'll find out about my Glock, too."

"You own a Glock?"

"I do. It's legal and registered. Nine mil. They haven't asked for it yet, but I'm guessing they will."

"Why do you have a pistol?"

"I've done some exposés, and the people I named weren't happy about it. Threats are just threats most of the time, but you never know. I don't have all that much faith in my fellow man. Bad things can happen."

"I understand that. Where were you when Brad was shot?"

"Working. I was in downtown Raleigh, trying to

find a source for a story I'm writing. I didn't find him. I didn't talk to anyone. I have no real alibi."

"That keeps you in the suspect pool."

"Don't I know it. But I would never kill Brad, not ever; not even in a fit of anger. You have to believe that, and you have to help me find the real killer."

Hope studied Chuck for a few seconds. She thought he was sincere, but how could she know? He had a pistol, and he didn't have an alibi. He was the jealous type, and he had fought with Brad in the past. Chuck made an ideal suspect.

"Like I told you, I'm not part of the investigation, but I will do what I can, which is not much. The police will have all the evidence."

"Thank you. I know you're hamstrung at the moment, but I have faith in you. In fact, if this all works out, I'd like to do a magazine item on you. The Sherlock Holmes of the South. How does that sound?"

"Like nonsense. I have no need for any publicity. I'm not in the business."

"As you wish, but it's there, if you want it."

"Perhaps when I'm older."

He laughed. "We all think we're going to be doing great things when we're older."

On the drive back to the farmhouse, Hope wondered how she was going to fulfill her commitment to Chuck. She was out of the information loop. What could she do to change that?

Nothing.

She was on the outside until Detective Robinson invited her in.

Simple, and frustrating.

Hope found Cori and Norrie in the music room. Norrie sat at the piano. Cori stood next to the older woman.

"This looks cozy," Hope said. "All went well?"

"Terrific," Cori said.

"Your daughter has a splendid voice, but I think you already know that," Norrie said.

"Can you make it better?" Hope asked.

"No, but I can help Cori make it better. That is, if she would like to work with me."

"I really liked our session, but I have some interviews with other coaches," Cori told the woman.

"I'm aware of that. When you've made a decision, please call. I simply wish to know the outcome."

"I'll definitely call," Cori said.

Norrie escorted them out the front door. Hope couldn't help but admire the grace of the older woman, and she wondered just how one acquired such poise.

"I like her," Cori said as soon as the car started.

"I know. I like her, too," Hope said. "She's a rather imposing person, isn't she?"

"She's very cool. No wonder she had all those photos on the walls."

"Do you want to keep interviewing?"

Cori frowned. "I think I should. I want to be sure I fit well with the coach. Does that make sense?"

"It does make sense. When you get home, write out the pluses and minuses about Norrie. Then, you can compare those to anyone else you interview. It's always good to have some kind of logic behind your choice. Feelings can sometimes be misleading."

"As you continue to remind me. And I agree. We'll do another interview tomorrow."

"Works for me. The sooner we complete the search, the sooner you choose a coach."

At home, Cori retreated to her room to create the reasons why she should or shouldn't choose Norrie. Hope was on her way to the kitchen when someone pounded on the front door. She and Bijou went to see who it was.

"Hello, Virginia," Hope said. "What—"

Virginia stormed past. "No time for a chat. Let me do the talking."

Hope stared. "What about?"

"Walt is dead. I have to confess before the police come."

14

Virginia stopped in the middle of the family room and faced Hope. "I know how this sounds, but please, remember that I'm your colleague and friend."

Hope crossed her arms over her chest. "Go on."

"Walt is dead. I'll start there."

"How do you know that?"

"I watched him die."

Hope was too stunned to ask a question. She simply continued staring.

"This will sound crazy. I mean, I know how it sounds, how it looks. I was asleep. I'm not quite sure how or why I fell asleep. I suspect Walt drugged me. I was in bed, and he woke me. I was ... am still groggy, a little. He called 911, which confused me. He was already coughing and panting, and he threw up as he told the 911 person that his wife had poisoned him."

"He said that?"

"More than once. He was smiling as he said it. I remember his lips were blue. He was dying. I get that now."

"Go on."

"He said that I had already killed my lover, and I was now killing him. That's crazy. I didn't kill Brad."

"Wait, wait, he knew about Brad?"

Virginia nodded. "I ... it's all so crazy. I didn't kill Brad. You have to believe that, Hope. I didn't shoot Brad, and I didn't poison Walt. That's insane."

"Why did he say you did?"

"I ... I can only guess that he killed Brad and then himself. Revenge ... it had to be revenge because I cheated."

"You do understand how unlikely that sounds, right?"

"I know, I know, but I can't think of anything else."

"You didn't wait for the police to arrive?"

"How could I? Walt collapsed right in front of me, and I heard him tell the 911 person that I had poisoned him. I had to get out of there."

Virginia paced, frowning and mumbling. Hope watched, wondering if she was suffering some kind of mental breakdown.

"Are you certain you heard Walt correctly? I mean, you said you had been asleep."

Virginia stopped and frowned. "I know what I heard. Don't tell me you believe him. I would never harm anyone."

"Right now, I don't know what to believe. I think you know that."

"I know that you're my only hope. The police are going to discover that Walt was poisoned. I have no idea how they might connect me to Brad's murder, but they will. They record all emergency calls, don't they?"

"I believe so, but, Virginia, I don't know how I can help you."

"You can't let Walt get away with this. He'll send me to prison for murders I didn't commit."

Hope wanted to debate the assumption that Walt had orchestrated the deaths of himself and Brad, but she didn't have time. The knock on the door drew her attention, and she went to open it.

"Is she here?" Detective Robinson asked. "Virginia Zalar. Her Tesla is parked in front."

"She's here."

"May I come in?"

Hope opened the door wide, and the detective moved past.

"You don't need a gun," Hope said as the detective's hand moved to his holster. "She's not armed ... as far as I can see."

He nodded, and she followed him into the family room where Virginia stood, her face unreadable.

"Virginia Zalar?" the detective asked.

She nodded.

"Would you mind coming with me to the station? I think we should talk."

"Am I under arrest?"

"Not yet, but that can be arranged."

"No, no, no need for that." Virginia turned to Hope. "Please help me. I don't have anyone on my side."

The detective turned to Hope. "Do I need to talk to you?"

Hope nodded. "I think so. After you interview Virginia."

He nodded. "I'll call you."

Hope watched as Virginia's face turned to stone. The woman was no longer readable, leaving Hope in a quandary. Was she supposed to dream up some sort of investigation? Was she obligated to help

Virginia? The way things stood, Virginia appeared to be the best suspect for Brad's death. Her confession about having an affair put her at the top of the list. Brad was not faithful to anyone, and jealousy was a wicked master. Walt had implicated Virginia. Would he lie? Why did Virginia flee when Walt called for help? Wasn't that another damning detail? Was Virginia for real, or was she just trying to muddy the waters before she went to trial? Hope couldn't tell.

"What was that about?"

Hope turned to Max, who seemed decidedly perplexed. "I'm not sure." She went on to explain how Virginia came to the door in order to convince her to investigate the deaths of Brad and Walter.

"She's grasping at straws," Max said. "Her own husband accused her."

"True, yet she denies it. I wonder what else the police will discover about her involvement."

"I was listening." Cori stepped into the room with the cat by her side.

Hope turned to her daughter. "And?"

"It sounds like some kind of mystery book. You know, the kind where everyone lies. The detective has to sort it out and find the truth."

Bijou let out a long hiss.

"Facts, Cori, facts. The facts go against Mrs. Zalar."

"Are you going to help her?"

"I don't know. I'll talk to Detective Robinson. I think he'll share what he's discovered. That will help me make a decision."

"Good luck."

Hope started for the kitchen. "Did you start your list of pluses and minuses?"

"I did. Not much so far. Tomorrow, we interview another coach."

"We do indeed."

Before bedtime, Hope climbed to her attic office and found Max busy with his computer.

"Another editing job?" Hope asked.

"Yes, and this one is not a good one either. The man is a tyrant. Nothing pleases him. If he knows so much about editing, why doesn't he edit his own work?"

"A second pair of eyes is often a good thing."

"Only if they're not hectored to death."

"No one likes a critic."

Max laughed. "Indeed."

The next day's interview was with a man who owned a small studio in Wilmington. Bearded and thin, with earrings and tattoos, he looked more like a drug pusher than voice coach. He did offer the plus of a recording studio. Cori was able to hear her recorded voice, but Hope was pretty sure the coaching was simply a side hustle. Dr. Z, as he called himself, was in the recording business. That would always take precedence over voice lessons.

"Nope," Cori said as soon as Hope started the engine.

"You're not going to work out the pluses and minuses?"

"Did you see the way he looked at you? Mom, that guy is a lecher. I'm half afraid to be alone with him."

"It might be just an act. He has to project a certain air."

"He can project that on someone else."

"Fair enough. Another one tomorrow?"

"Roger that."

Hope's phone chirped, and she glanced at the ID. "Do we know Thad Overman?"

"Nope."

"In that case, I'll see if he leaves a message. Pizza tonight? I don't feel like cooking."

"Works for me. Can I invite Lottie?"

"Sure, and her mother. You girls can have your own table."

Cori grinned and grabbed her phone.

～

It was early evening when Hope looked across the table, where Lottie's mother sipped her red wine.

"I don't get it," Adele said. "The wine here never tastes the same from one week to the next. I grow accustomed to a certain flavor, and before I know it, the wine has been changed."

"They do it on purpose," Hope said, "just to vex you."

"If the pizza weren't so good, I'd find another place. Tell me about Virginia Zalar."

"There's nothing to tell," Hope said reaching for her own glass of wine.

"Don't try that line on me. You're the ace detective here. You're in the know."

Hope smiled, remembering how she had once helped Adele avoid a murder charge. Since that dust up, Adele had come to believe that Hope always knew what the police knew.

"I really don't know. Since Cori and I found Brad's body, I have been shut out of that investigation. Virginia's arrest appears to be an extension of that first killing. So, I'm still out of the loop."

"But she came to you, right? She must have said she was innocent."

"She did, but she couldn't prove it. I'm not certain the police can prove she had anything to do with Brad's murder or the death of her husband. They aren't sharing."

"I heard that he said she poisoned him. Is that true?"

Hope nodded. "I think so. I can't say for certain."

"Why would he do that if it wasn't true?"

"I have no idea."

"Did he know she was cheating?"

"I don't know that either."

Adele looked around the room as if checking for eavesdroppers. She leaned across the table, a conspirator. "Here's what I think. I think Virginia killed Brad. Walter found out about Virginia, and he threatened to turn her in. That makes sense. Who wants to sleep with a murderer? He figured it out before he died. She didn't have a chance to cremate the body. He did make a 911 call, right?"

"He did."

"That is so damning, right? I mean who does that to his wife if it's not true?"

Hope shook her head. "No one that I know."

"Exactly. So, she has to be guilty."

"Not till it's been proven. Remember, in our system, the accused gets to question the accuser in court."

"That's not gonna happen. He's dead."

"Yes, but he'll speak through the facts and evidence that's presented. She'll have the opportunity to question that."

Adele drummed her fingers on the red and white checked table top. "You don't think I should decide without knowing more, right?"

"No, I happen to agree with you. It looks like she killed them both, and she's trying to add some confusion so she doesn't go to prison."

"What do we still need to know?"

"I'm not sure. I'm guessing she would need access to a firearm like the one that killed Brad, and I think the police would like to tie her to the poison that killed Walter. If they can't do that, all they really have is Walter's accusation. That could be the last gasp of a dying man whose wife betrayed her marriage vows."

"You make it sound so clinical. Doesn't rage fit in there someplace?"

"Oh, I think emotions played a big role. How could they not? But, we don't know anything about that. I'm ready to move on to another topic. How is

Lottie doing these days?"

"She wants voice lessons." Adele laughed. "She can't sing at all; really bad, like her mother. But, if Cori is going to get lessons, Lottie wants them, too."

"That seems like a waste of money. Doesn't she have some other talent to pursue?"

"Believe it or not, she has an eye for fashion. Now, that's something I can support."

"Talk her into design lessons?"

"I'll do my best, but you know teenage girls. They suddenly know more than their parents, lots more. Listening is for kids."

When the pizzas arrived, Hope made eye contact with Cori, who held up a thumb. The pizza passed muster.

"Did you ever wonder why Virginia married Walter?" Adele asked, her mouth half full of pepperoni pizza.

"I've never really thought about it," Hope answered.

"Well, he was quite a bit older. As far as I know, he didn't have a lot of money, and he wasn't particularly handsome. She's attractive. You would think she could find a better catch."

"Do people still use that term? I mean, 'catching' a husband is a thing of the past, isn't it?"

"Hope, no wonder you're still single. Modern women do an asset check before they marry. It's a lot easier to have a good marriage if you're not arguing about the rent money."

"Can you learn to love someone?"

"Well, you need some basic compatibility. I mean, he can't have smelly feet, and he has to pick up his own clothes, but with time, you learn to overlook the small things that annoy you. I mean, if that's the worst thing about a spouse, then you have a pretty good spouse."

"I sometimes think that's what makes marriage attractive to older people. They're past all the heavy sex part. They can simply enjoy each other's company."

"No, no, no, Hope. You're not that old. Don't ever think that way. I think you need to take a singles cruise. You know, with all those hunks running around."

Hope laughed. "Just what I need, a boatload of egomaniacs." Her phone chirped.

"Who is it?" Adele asked.

"Thad Overman."

"Who's he?"

"I'm guessing he's Virginia's attorney."

15

The man entered Hope's classroom before the final bell signaled dismissal. The students turned, looking at the older man who wore a short-sleeve white shirt and a blue tie with his khaki pants. He nodded at Hope and moved to the back, standing against the wall. The final minutes were generally a time for students to chat—provided they had been respectful. It was a small reward Hope used to maintain discipline.

When the bell rang, the students quickly filed out. They were still chatting, and they paid no attention to the man with white hair and a slight stoop. When they were gone, he pushed off the wall and smiled.

"Good afternoon, Mrs. Herring," he said. "I'm Thad Overman, Virginia's attorney."

"Good afternoon. How is Virginia?"

"As good as can be expected. Do you mind if we talk outside?"

Hope was a bit surprised. "Why?"

"I'm old fashioned and a bit paranoid. Law enforcement doesn't always play by the rules, if you know what I mean. I hate to have my conversations recorded and played back in court. It's embarrassing. I just like to be careful."

Hope smiled. "Let me gather my things."

Minutes later, Hope and Thad stood on the sidewalk in front of the school. The yellow buses were mostly full and beginning to ooze out of the parking lot. A line of cars snaked past the building—moms and dads picking up the children who didn't ride the bus. The sun was still bright; a fine afternoon.

"I never rode the bus," Thad said. "We lived about a mile from school, and my parents believed the walk would do me good. They were right, mostly. Although, there were some frosty mornings when I would have appreciated a ride."

"The students don't walk anymore. It's a safety issue. They're better off on the bus, even if it's a short ride," Hope explained.

"Sometimes, I think we're raising scaredy cats. Is it any wonder that today's children suffer mental disorders?"

"It's the media. Parents think dozens of children are kidnapped every day. They're not, of course, but the children who are taken get a lot of time on the news channels."

"A sign of our times, I'm afraid. Mrs. Herring, I represent Virginia Zalar, and she indicated she had asked you to look into the charges against her."

"She did, but I told her and I'll tell you that I don't have access to police files. My daughter and I found the body of Brad Edie. I was excluded from any part of the investigation."

"I'm aware of that. I'm also aware that you are the foremost detective in North Carolina."

"Hardly. I've helped the police on some cases, but they did all the hard work."

"Don't be overly modest. You've done great work. Everyone knows that. I'm not sure what you can do for Virginia, but I'm following her wishes. She wants you to know what I know and what the police have revealed to us. I'm afraid many damning facts have come to light. She is in great jeopardy."

"I suspected as much. What can you tell me?"

"Then, you're going to look into things?"

"I'll do what I can. If things are as clearcut as you seem to think, then I won't be able to help her."

"I'll start with the Edie murder, as you are a bit familiar with that one. According to the coroner's report, Brad was killed with a Glock semi-automatic pistol. No need to go into the bloody details. The wound was not self-inflicted. He did not commit suicide. The pistol was not recovered at the scene. Virginia's house was searched. The police found a Glock pistol. Virginia admitted that the firearm belonged to her. It seems Walter had been spooked by the number of burglaries in the area. He acquired the gun and gave it to his wife. They would practice shooting together. She knew how to use the weapon."

"I presume they did ballistics on the Glock?"

"The state police lab performed the test. The weapon matched the recovered bullet. There were no shell casings recovered from the murder site, so there was nothing to match there. Fingerprints were mostly smudged on the weapon, but the prints that were viable belonged to Virginia. The prints on the magazine were also hers, as were the ones on the cartridges. They found no other prints. While Virginia maintains that she did not shoot Mr. Edie, the forensic evidence says she did. No powder residue was found on her hands or clothes, but then, they were not examined until sometime after the murder."

"Tell me, you said she practiced with her husband. What sort of firearm did he have?"

"He also had a Glock, which was tested. It was not the murder weapon. He also possessed a thirty-eight-caliber revolver and a twelve-gauge, pump shotgun. The police possess all the weapons at this time."

"What else do they have?"

"I don't know if Virginia told you, but her alibi is that she was home asleep when the murder was committed. That has been called into question by camera footage."

"What?" Hope's eyes widened. "How so?"

"Her Tesla, which is rather distinctive if you recall, was caught by two cameras, both on a route to Edie's residence. There are no witnesses that saw the car at his house, but the hour was late and he lived in a secluded location."

"I know. I've been there."

"While the car, which was positively identified, is proof enough, one of the cameras, caught a brief glimpse of the driver. About all that can be seen is a lot of blond hair. Virginia is blond. The only prints in the car were hers and her husband's. That doesn't prove she was driving, but it sort of rules out a lot of other people."

"And Walter is dead, so he can't provide an alibi."

"Her firearm provides the means. Her car going back and forth at roughly the time of the murder provides opportunity. That brings us to motive. Why would Virginia kill Brad Edie?"

"She admitted that they were having an affair?" Hope asked.

"She did. She also said it was mostly over. According to her, it was one of those affairs of opportunity. They worked together, and he, apparently, was some sort of seducer. If the stories are true, he had had many partners before he was with Virginia."

"If the affair was mostly over, why would she kill him?"

"I believe the police are working on the theory that she was being blackmailed. Edie wanted money, and he threatened to expose her unless she paid up."

"That doesn't sound like Virginia. She was the type to call his bluff and let things fall where they would. Besides, Walter wasn't some kind of millionaire. A divorce might be nasty, but it would not turn her into a beggar."

"Exactly. However, the police found a bundle of cash hidden in Edie's bedroom—under a loose floorboard, if I'm not mistaken. Her prints are on the top and bottom bills, exactly what you would expect if she handed over the cash."

"No other prints?"

"None identified."

"Not even Brad's?"

He shook his head. "That seems odd, but he might have been careful."

"That's her motive then."

Thad nodded. "Which brings us to the next death ... Walter Zalar."

"Means?"

"Poison. He ingested a rather large dose of fast-acting poison, apparently in a salami sandwich. Walter liked salami, and Virginia regularly fixed him sandwiches. When he discovered he had been poisoned, he called 911. I've listened to the recording. He clearly says his wife poisoned him. He also says she killed Brad Edie. By the time the police arrived, he was dead and she was gone. I believe she visited you, where she was arrested."

"She did. I can tell you that she denied killing Brad or her husband. She overheard him on the 911 call. She also recognized that he was beyond help. That was why she ran."

"Did you tell her you would help?"

"I made no commitment. I told her the truth. I was not privy to the information you have. After listening to you, I don't think I can help her. What do the police know about the poison?"

"The poison came in pill form, which she reduced to a powder. They think she added the powder to the mustard she used in the sandwich. She says she knows nothing about the pills, powder, or mustard. Unfortunately, the police found several additional pills in a prescription pill bottle with her name on it. The poison was mixed in with another medication. Only her prints are on the bottle. Either she forgot she hid them there, or she missed them."

"Her explanation?"

"She knows nothing about the poison. She has no idea how they popped up in her pill bottle. The police are having trouble finding the source, as you might expect."

Hope watched the last of the cars pull away from the school. "Is there any evidence on her side?"

"Very little. There is no direct evidence that Edie was blackmailing her. No notes, no phone messages. Of course, a smart man wouldn't put such demands in writing. Again, no one watched her reduce the pills to powder and lace Walter's sandwich. I don't think I need to tell you how Walter's phone call will sound in court. She's looking at considerable prison time."

"Why would Walter say that if it wasn't true?"

Thad shrugged. "Virginia doesn't know and won't speculate. According to her, their married life, while not overly exciting was still pretty good. She insists Edie was the only person she cheated with. She also says Walter never cheated on her. I don't think the police are looking too hard for Walter's paramour. Again, according to Virginia, Walter liked his work, and he had a very viable and rewarding hobby."

"The paintings?"

"Exactly. I was wondering if they might be so valuable, that she would kill him for the art. I'm not quick to bring that up, as it might provide further evidence of motive. She would inherit whatever value they had."

Hope shook her head. "I don't see how I can help her or you. I mean, it appears that the police have a tight case."

"They do. I would suggest that when you talk to Virginia, and she intends to talk to you, try to implant the idea of a plea bargain. If they offer manslaughter instead of murder, that would be a big reduction in the sentence."

"Manslaughter?"

"The truth might be that she made the poison powder in order to get rid of a pesky racoon or possum or some other unwelcome animal. She accidentally spilled some on Walter's sandwich. That might work."

"If she were to admit to that."

"She's not inclined at the moment."

"You've informed her of the evidence against her?"

"I have. She says it's not evidence at all. No one saw her do anything. No one spotted her at Edie's house. No one watched her pulverize pills. It's all some clever plot to frame her for the murders."

"Clever plot perpetrated by whom?"

He shrugged. "I asked if she had enemies, and she said no one who would go to such extremes."

"Who gets the art if she goes to prison?"

"Whoever she gives it to. Walter didn't leave any instructions."

"More motive."

"I'm not asking you to do anything but talk to her. Frankly, if she goes to trial, I don't see a way to defend her. She could plead temporary insanity, but that rarely works. She doesn't strike anyone as being mentally ill."

"I'll do what I can," Hope said, "but like you, I don't see a lot of holes in the case. While no one saw her commit murder, no one was with her when the murders occurred."

"I'm glad we had this chat, Mrs. Herring. I think you have a chance to explain what this all means. I did my best, but Virginia insists she's innocent. She wants a trial." Thad smiled, nodded, and walked away.

Hope stared after him. He had not painted a pretty picture. All the evidence ran against Virginia. He knew it, and now, Hope knew it.

Cori arrived, all smiles.

"Ready for the next interview?" Hope asked.

"Nope," Cori answered. "I've decided that I don't need any more. I want Norrie to coach me."

"You're sure?"

"I am. More interviewing would be a waste of time."

"We certainly don't want that." Hope smiled.

Max met Hope as soon as she walked into the house.

"I think I might have a problem," the ghost said.

16

Max pointed to the computer screen which was filled with red letters that spelled RANSOM. Underneath was a list of instructions that demanded payment in order for the computer to be unlocked.

"I've tried all the keys," Max said. "Nothing works."

"This happened once before. Remember we pulled the plug?"

"Pulled the plug?"

"We pulled the plug to kill the power," Hope told him.

"Oh yes, that's right, but it says that I shouldn't do that," Max pointed out.

"Well, sure it does. What would we expect it to

say? They certainly don't want to tell you how to bypass the lock."

"Of course, you're right. Why didn't I think of that?"

"The first response is usually panic. People don't want to lose what's on their computer, although the files on this one are nothing to worry about. We lose some photos or letters or whatever, and it's no big deal. Besides, this computer is backed up to the cloud once or twice a week. We can recover everything except for the last day or so."

"What about my editing?"

"Oh, I forgot about that. I'm afraid that you might have to start over."

Max moaned. "I've spent a lot of hours editing."

"I'm not saying that will happen. Many programs automatically save to the hard drive after so many minutes. There's a good chance the file will be recovered with minimal loss."

"I so hope that's the case." Max looked worried.

"Do you mind telling me how it managed to get locked?"

"I was being stupid. I know better than to go for clickbait. I was surfing, resting for a few minutes. One of those strange ads popped onto the screen. I believe it was something about making a lot of money. I know, I know, what would I do with a lot of money? It was stupid. I clicked it. This is the result."

"I don't think there's been any harm. Are you ready for the experiment?"

"Experiment?"

"Pulling the plug. First, however, I'm going to try a warm boot."

"Warm boot?"

"Restarting the computer is called booting. You can reboot without turning off the power by pressing control, alt, delete all at once. That restarts the machine."

Hope sat and pressed the three keys.

The only thing that happened was a loud "SCREE" from the computer.

"Sorry about that," Hope said. "I was afraid they had programmed for that particular effort."

"It's like the computer is wounded."

Hope laughed. "I suppose it does sound like that." She rose and went to the wall, where she pulled a plug from a socket. As soon as she did, the "SCREE" ceased.

"This is called a cold boot because the computer is completely shut down cold. Now, we'll wait for a couple of minutes to make sure no residual energy remains. Then, we'll turn it on again."

"I apologize for causing such trouble."

"Nonsense, Max, we all do it. Every time you click on a site or ad, you take a chance."

Hope plugged in the cord and returned to the computer. She put her finger on the on/off button.

"Ready?"

"If I have broken your computer, I will find a way to replace it."

"No need. You didn't do anything wrong."

Hope switched on the computer and waited. She and Max stared at the screen.

"Come on," Max muttered. "Come on."

Even as they watched, the familiar computer logo filled the screen.

"There you go," Hope said. "I think everything will be fine. Although you may have to redo some of your editing."

"Gladly, gladly, thank you so much. I shall never succumb to my urges again."

"Never say never, Max." Hope laughed.

After leaving the attic, Hope found Cori in the kitchen, busy with her homework.

"Did you save Max?" Cori asked.

"Yep. He made the mistake of clicking on the wrong ad and allowing ransomware to grab the computer. Luckily, it was more for show than anything else. We did a cold boot, and the computer came back. All is well."

"That's great. Just to let you know, I called Norrie and asked her to be my voice coach. She said yes. Tomorrow, if that's all right with you."

"It's fine, and thank you."

"Thank me? Why would you thank me?"

"Because you took responsibility for your lessons. That's a big step. It's part of growing up. In a way, I'm sorry about that. I'd like to keep you my little girl."

"If you did that, I wouldn't need teachable moments."

Hope laughed, and the doorbell rang. "I'll get that. Keep working."

Hope opened the door to find Detective Robinson smiling back at her.

"I hate to ask," he began, "but could you come down to the station and talk to Virginia Zalar?"

"Now?"

"She's been asking for you, and, well, I think she might become more cooperative if she can talk to you."

"I can't advise her. You know that."

"I'm not asking you to. You talked to Thad today?"

"I did."

"And, he told you about all the evidence we've gathered? The weapon, the poison?"

"He did, and I'll say that you've put together quite a strong case."

"We think so. I mean, the dominoes all line up. There aren't many holes for the defense to exploit."

"It sounded that way."

"That's all I want you to tell Virginia. You can give her all the facts Thad told you. I think that once she learns that we've got the goods on her, she'll make things easy for all of us and confess."

Hope looked wary. "I can't tell her to do that."

"Of course not, but you can reason with her. You can show her just how precarious her position is."

"I'll talk to her, but I make no promises. If she's guilty, I hope she'll try to work a deal."

"There aren't many deals available for a double homicide."

"We can only do the best we can."

Before she left for the police station, Hope made Cori promise to stay inside and finish her work. Max would be there, so Cori would be more than safe. She hoped her ride to the station wouldn't be in vain.

Hope noticed the change in Virginia as soon as the woman walked into the room. Nothing about Virginia was as bright as it had been; not her hair, not her eyes, not her skin, nothing. She looked as if she had been dipped in ashes—pale and dull. She sat heavily and forced a smile.

"Thank you for coming," Virginia said. "I've been going crazy. I have no one to talk to, no one to cry with. I can't even mourn properly. Brad was one thing. Walter was quite another. I need to get out of here and take care of his funeral."

"Has the body been released?"

"Not that I'm aware of."

"When it is, let me know. If you'd like me to, I can see to the funeral and burial."

"No, Hope, I don't want you to do that. That's my job. I need to get out of here and take care of my dead husband."

Hope's voice was serious. "I'm not so sure that is going to happen any time soon."

"I didn't kill anyone, Hope. I'm innocent."

"I don't doubt that, but do you know how much evidence the police have accumulated?"

"What? All that stuff about my gun being used? I

can't explain that. I don't know how someone managed to get my gun and kill Brad with it. Are they absolutely sure it was my Glock?"

Hope nodded. "It was yours. The gun had your prints on it, along with the magazine and cartridges. How do you explain that?"

"Gloves, of course. My prints had to be on the gun. It's mine."

"Yes, but how did the killer acquire it? Did you know it was missing?"

"The Glock isn't something I check on daily. It could go missing for weeks, and I wouldn't know."

"Walter?"

"He wouldn't know either. We never pulled out the firearms unless we were going shooting."

"All right, who had access to your house?"

"Our maid service, some repairmen probably. Friends and neighbors. We did entertain occasionally. It's not like we kept the guns locked up in a safe. They were kept in the closet, on a shelf."

"Who knew about them?"

"I don't have a list. I mean, there were several times Walt pulled them out and showed them to our friends. He was proud of the Glocks, and he was a good shot."

"Did he know about Brad and you?"

"I didn't think he knew, but I'm really not sure. Walter was meek, but I don't think he was someone who would accept infidelity. I think he would have confronted me."

"He didn't?"

Virginia shook her head. "Not a peep. Maybe he knew and was biding his time about confronting me."

"Okay, someone took your gun and your car, drove to Brad's, and shot him. Who could do that? And, the person has to be blond. The security cameras prove that much."

"I wish I could tell you. I can't. Someone pretended to be me. I know about the cameras. I never went that way. I don't think the police can find another instance of my car passing the camera."

"Walter?"

Virginia turned away. Hope could tell that the woman was fighting the obvious.

"If Walter didn't know about Brad, why would he pretend to be you?"

"I don't know. I don't know, Hope. I've gone over things again and again. Walter is the only person that makes sense, and he doesn't make sense. Nothing makes sense."

"Was Brad blackmailing you?"

"What? Brad? No, nothing like that. We had ... slowed down. That hurt a little but not that much. He wasn't the kind to blackmail anyone. There were too many people out there who knew too much about him."

"I believe you. I liked Brad. I never thought he was that type, but the police are working on that theory. They want to tell the jury you paid him cash before you killed him."

"That is crazy. If I was going to kill him, I certainly wouldn't give him money."

"You might if you wanted him to feel at ease when you showed up."

Virginia shook her head. "Don't go there. I'm not that calculating."

"Someone is. All right, let's talk about Walter. If you didn't poison him, who did?"

Virginia rubbed her face and tapped the table with her fist. "I know how that looks. They found the pills in one of my bottles. They figured out how the poison was delivered. Walter accused me of the poisoning over the phone. He believed I had done it. I can accept that now. Who else would he accuse?"

"Who were his enemies?"

"No one who would kill him. I mean, he had spats with some men, but no battles or threats."

"Who gains from his death?"

Virginia pulled a tired smile. "Me. That's as it should be, right? He had life insurance, lots of life insurance. That's mine. The house is mine. Everything is mine. So, unless there's something I'm missing, I'm in trouble."

"Are you certain?"

Virginia nodded. "I'm sure the district attorney has figured that out by now."

"Is there any reason Walter would kill himself?"

"Walter wasn't the suicidal type. He wasn't old or senile. He wasn't in trouble financially. Why would he poison himself? I'll add that the death was painful, very painful. If he were going to kill himself, he would use a Glock. Quick and reasonably painless."

"It would also not implicate you."

She frowned. "You think Walter wanted the police to think it was me?"

"I don't know what to think, Virginia. Let's face it, all the evidence points to you. Your denials are just that … denials. You have no alibis. You can't even offer a viable alternative. Frankly, I have a hard time believing you. The facts don't support you."

"If you don't believe me…" Virginia hung her head.

Hope reached across and took Virginia's hand, even though she wasn't supposed to do that.

"I want you to think back," Hope said. "Did Walter do anything out of the ordinary during the last six months? Any new habits? Any old habits given up? New friends or enemies? Sleep issues? Anything?"

"No, nothing. He was always good old Walter. There was the prostate thing, but that didn't seem to be life-threatening."

Hope stared at the woman. Walter had denied having cancer, but Virginia claimed that he did. She decided not to press the issue right then. "I want you to think about it. I mean really think. If you come up with anything, call me."

"You ... you think I should try to work a deal, don't you?"

"I can't advise you on that. I'm not your attorney."

"He thinks that's the only option. They have too much evidence."

"Maybe you should listen to him."

"I'm innocent. I don't have to get a deal." Virginia began to cry.

Hope wanted to console the woman, but that was not the right thing to do, not right at all.

Max was sitting with Cori when Hope entered the kitchen. They looked perfectly at home with each other, both laughing. Hope wanted to join them, but she couldn't push away her thoughts of Virginia. What was Hope going to do for the woman?

17

The call came while Hope was waiting for Cori to finish her first voice lesson with Norrie. She looked at the ID, pushed her cart to the side of the grocery store aisle, and answered.

"Virginia?" Hope asked.

"Thank you for answering," Virginia said. "I don't have a lot of time, so I'll make this short. You asked if Walter had done anything odd in the months leading up to the poisoning. Well, he did. About six months ago, he drove to Raleigh three times. Twice, he stayed overnight. I didn't think anything of it since I was seeing Brad. Walter being away made it easier for us. I know how that sounds, but it's the truth. I was ... foolish."

"You don't know why he went?"

"He said it was a business deal, and it fell through. That's all I know. Like I said, I didn't want any details."

"Any idea who he saw or where he stayed?"

"No. I was distracted by my own stupidity."

"All right. Records. Would there be a record of his trips?"

"I'm guessing yes. If he was going to use it as a business expense, he would have to post it."

"How can we find out?"

"He did most of his own bookkeeping, but he did have an accountant who helped monthly and filed the quarterly taxes. His name is George Barrow. He has an office in Wilmington."

"You'll have to contact him and tell him to let me see Walter's books."

"I can do that. Do you really think it will help?"

"No, I won't lead you on. I'm pretty sure it's just what Walter told you, a business deal that didn't pan out."

"Yeah, I thought so, but you'll take a look?"

"I will. I'll let you know if I find anything."

"Thank you."

Hope ended the connection and wondered if she was being used. Was Virginia sending her on a fruitless mission, simply to blast some chaff into the air? It was a distraction, something her attorney might be able to use to confuse the jury. Virginia was more than bright enough to figure that out. With a sigh, Hope pushed the cart forward. She still had shopping to finish.

When she entered the attic office, Hope found Max positively gleeful. He jumped out of the chair and danced around the room.

"I've finished it," he announced, "and my work has been approved. The money will soon be deposited. I could not be happier."

"Congratulations. Are you now the editor of choice for a lot of clients?"

"No, no, I don't think so. In fact, I might try ghostwriting instead of editing. I mean, I have read widely. I should be able to turn out a passable story."

"Well, as a ghostwriter, you don't have to curse any bad reviews."

He laughed. "I never thought of that, but you're correct. I will get paid no matter what the readers think."

"Don't do a bad job, or you won't get more work."

"Mrs. Herring, I shall try my utmost to be the best I can be. I trust that will be good enough."

"I'm sure it will be. You're a man of letters. You'll do fine."

At the dinner table, Cori posed a question.

"Do you mind if I spend Saturday afternoon with Norrie?" Cori asked.

"Of course not, but I need to know what you'll be doing."

"Not practicing. I have to be mindful of my voice. She wants to watch several musicals with me. She wants to point out certain techniques that I have to learn. It's all part of the lesson plan, so it won't cost extra."

Hope nodded. "You really like her, don't you?"

"You know, I do. She's very interesting. When she has me try something, she tells me who did it before me. You know, another singer. She says there's nothing in singing that hasn't been done before. Some people did it better than others, but there's nothing new."

"She's probably right. To get something original, I think you'll have to add electronics. A computer might be able to alter the sound."

"That might work, but I don't want to go that way. I want to use my own voice."

"Exactly. Since you're going to be busy, I'm going

to Wilmington. I need to see an accountant who might be able to help Mrs. Zalar."

"Everyone at school says she's way guilty. I heard that Mr. Zalar said that over the phone to the 911 dispatcher."

"He did, but that doesn't make it true. Since he's dead, his wife can't question him about it either."

"Do you think she's guilty?"

"I think there's a lot of evidence that points to her guilt. That won't keep me from following up on any leads she might provide. Every dead end helps."

"Dead ends help?"

"I think it was Sherlock Holmes who said that after all impossible theories are discounted, what remains, no matter how improbable, must be the truth."

Cori shrugged. "Sometimes, it's none of the above."

Hope laughed. "Indeed, it is."

Saturday afternoon traffic was not the worst Hope had ever encountered, but it was slow enough, especially with the rain that had settled over the city. A storm system was moving up the coast, and such weather always produced a fair amount of moisture. Given a choice, she would have put off the appointment. Yet, George Barrow had agreed to meet her, and Virginia was still wasting away in jail. She wasn't going to quit.

George's office occupied a small space in a mostly vacant strip mall off Market Street. No doubt, the strip had been popular at one time, but open-air malls across town had drawn off traffic. Hope could tell that the strip was struggling. FOR RENT signs were plastered on the windows.

The door was locked, and Hope was forced to knock. She had to wait a few seconds before a large man unlocked the door for her.

"Come in, come in," the round man said. "I apologize for the locked door, but this isn't the best of neighborhoods." He locked the door behind her. "Everyone feels a little better with the door locked. You must be Hope Herring, the ace detective."

"I am Hope Herring, but I'm hardly an ace detective."

"Don't be so modest. Come on back to my office."

He led her past what would have been a reception area on a full workday. His inner office was more warehouse, with no windows or doors. The furnishings were passable, but they were not what a big-time accounting firm would offer. His desk was large and wooden, and he settled into a big, worn leather chair.

"All right," he began as she sat. "I talked briefly with Virginia, so I'm roughly aware of what you're looking for. Mind being a little more detailed?"

George was casually dressed in a white polo and jeans. His face had a ruddy tinge. Hope guessed he liked his beer, given his belly. She also guessed that he might have played football at some point.

"You're aware that most of the evidence the police have collected points to Virginia as the murderer of both Brad Edie and her husband, Walter."

"She mentioned that, but she wasn't specific. I take it they have a strong case?"

"Very strong. Her gun, her husband's accusation, and traffic camera footage, a lot of it points directly at her."

"That's too bad. I always liked Virginia. I liked Walter, too, but he wasn't as much fun as she was."

"I agree with that. While the police have a lot, they don't have any witnesses that place Virginia at the scene of the crime."

"Traffic cameras?"

"The car and someone who might have been her. She claims she never took that route. The driver's face is not recognizable."

"So, you're thinking Walter framed her?"

"I don't see how anyone else could have done it. He had access to her firearm and her car. She claims she was asleep when Brad was killed, which means she might have been drugged."

"All right, Walter framed her for Brad. He was poisoned. He did that to himself?"

"It doesn't make sense, does it? I mean, if he's going to all that trouble to kill Brad, why wouldn't he just sit back and let the police put her in jail?"

"I didn't know Walter all that well. He was my client but not a close friend. I can tell you that he loved his wife. I can also tell you that he was a straight arrow. He believed that people needed to be punished for their sins. I wouldn't be too surprised if he thought Virginia should pay for cheating on him."

"Did he know about the cheating?"

"I have no idea, but I don't think he would kill himself. Walter liked the life he had."

"Before Virginia found another man?"

"Yeah, before that."

"So, if Walter did kill her lover and himself, the question is why."

George shrugged. "I have no idea. As far as I know, he was doing just fine. His business was good. Not spectacular, but making money. Not deep in debt. He lived what most people would consider an enviable life."

"Exactly. Virginia recalls three business trips he took to Raleigh about six months ago. He spent the night there twice. He told her it was a deal that didn't pan out. I was thinking that if it was a business deal, he would have posted the expenses. Since he was a detail man, he wouldn't have overlooked that."

"I must apologize for not remembering those exact dates and charges." He turned to his computer. "But, I should be able to pull up the money he spent. You're right about Walter, he charged everything he could to his business."

Hope waited while George worked the keyboard and mouse. The accountant was adept, and it was but a minute or two before he tapped his computer screen.

"Virginia has a good memory. It was five months ago. Three trips to Raleigh. Two one-night stays at a local motel."

"Any note about the reason for the trips?"

"No, nothing. That's odd."

"What's odd?" Hope asked.

He pointed to the screen again. "While the initial costs were expensed to the business, the costs were backed out one month later."

"Backed out?"

"Reversed. The net effect is zero, but in accounting, you can't just erase something. You have to reverse the credit with a debit."

"I see. Do you remember why he would do that?"

"I do. Well, I think I do. Walter isn't my only client, so my memory isn't perfect. As I recall, he came in one day and asked me to take the costs off the books. I think he said he had second thoughts. Since there had been no income to declare, he was afraid the IRS would want to dig a little deeper. I believe I argued that they were legitimate expenses, but he was adamant. He would feel better if he paid for the trips."

"You don't handle his personal accounts?"

George shook his head. "No, no, just the business. You'll have to go through Virginia, if you want to audit his personal expenses."

"I will, but no idea why he went to Raleigh?"

"None, sorry. I'm sure it was business. That's all I can say."

"Can you tell me who the payment was made to?"

"Want a cup of coffee? Because it will take me a few minutes to pull the original voucher."

"Where's the coffee?"

"There's a small room off the lobby. Coffee should still be hot."

"Thanks. I'll be right back."

Hope left the office and found the small canteen. The coffee was bitter, as it had been too hot for too long. Tannins were the culprit. She drank the coffee anyway.

When Hope walked back into the office, George handed her an envelope.

"I made copies of the vouchers. They're nothing special. Motel receipts, restaurants, gas. To me, it looked like he ate alone."

"Great, thanks. If you happen to remember anything else..."

"I'll call you."

The windshield wipers swiped back and forth as Hope drove back to Norrie's house. While Walter's trips to Raleigh turned out to be a bit odd, they certainly did not explain anything. He had charged some things to his business that he'd later had second thoughts about. Nothing suspicious about that. Better to avoid an IRS audit than to have to explain everything. Hope knew she would have to report to Virginia and ask the jailed woman if she could remember anything else about Walter's trips.

"She is really cool," Cori said as Hope drove away from Norrie's house.

"I'm glad you like her."

"I do, a lot. She told me I will soon need a manager."

"Did she have someone in mind?"

"She wants to discuss it with you."

18

Hope arrived home from having an early dinner with her casual boyfriend Luke Donlan. Luke owned a landscaping business, and having a stellar reputation for quality work, he was always in demand and always busy. Because neither one wanted to rush into anything, they were taking their relationship slow. They would meet for dinner or coffee, take a bike ride, or he would come to Hope's place to cook dinner with her and Cori. The two of them enjoyed each other's company and they could see moving forward together someday, but that day was way, way off in the distant future, and for now, Hope was happy with the way things were.

She sat at the kitchen table, her laptop open, and the voucher copies on the side. She stared at the photo of the Carolina Inn, which wasn't in Raleigh at all. It was in Chapel Hill, not far from the University of North Carolina campus. Walter spent two nights at the Inn, which made Hope wonder why he had told Virginia he was in Raleigh. Walter wasn't one to make a mistake, not twice. Once, maybe, but not twice. He had misled Virginia for a reason.

Why?

He didn't want her to know what he was doing.

Why?

Hope didn't believe for a minute that Walter was cheating on his cheating wife. He wasn't the type. He didn't possess the charm, looks, or money to pick up a pretty woman. So, what was he doing in Chapel Hill? Why did he spend two nights instead of three? Why didn't he go back? If it was a woman, why did it end? She couldn't figure it out.

The Carolina Inn.

Chapel Hill.

Hope knew she would have to make a trip to Chapel Hill and try to find out why Walter went there. After five months, she didn't think she would discover anything. Not unless Virginia knew more than she let on. Barring that, the best Hope was going to get was probably a recent photo of Walter, one she could show around.

Taking Chances

Would anyone recognize Walter?

Not likely.

Hope tapped the computer screen, muttering to herself. "What did you do, Walter? What did you do?"

Max appeared and sat across the table. "Good evening, Mrs. Herring. I must say that Cori is quite taken with her new coach. I hope you are equally pleased."

"I am, but I'm leery. I'm sure Norrie will coach well, but she's already spoken to Cori about getting a manager. I realize that managers are necessary in show business, but I was hoping Cori could avoid that for a year or two. Singing is one thing. Singing for money is another."

"I share your trepidation. In my day, most of the really good singers did so in church. They sang for the love of music, not to make money."

"Today, they go online to post songs on TikTok and other sites. They gather followers, who beg for more. The more followers, the more fame. Talent and charm spread out like a spider web. Talent hunters find those performers, and before you know it, a contract is signed. The talent goes to TV, online, or on stage. The game hasn't changed, just the delivery and the speed. It doesn't take years. People go from obscurity to fame to obscurity in between blue moons."

Max said, "I agree, as you tell the truth. Is there something I can do to help?"

"This is a teachable moment for me. Can I step back enough to allow Cori to make her own decisions? Will she come to me ... or you ... for advice? I would like that to happen before I have to step in and enforce something. Does that make sense?"

"It does. You are showing enviable restraint. I'm afraid I would have barreled in by now."

"I'm almost there now. Pray that I keep my cool."

~

The next afternoon, Detective Robinson accompanied Hope past the yellow crime tape that blocked the entrance into Virginia's house.

"You know you're chasing gremlins, right?" the detective asked.

"I know, and I keep telling myself I'm being stupid. I mean, Virginia isn't even that good of a friend."

"I think you like the challenge, Hope. I think you want to prove you can solve any mystery out there."

"Doesn't it bother you that there are no witnesses who saw Virginia do anything?"

The detective said, "No living witnesses. I'm guessing Walter saw a few things."

"Maybe."

"Look at it this way. What if Walter was the one asleep on the night his wife drove to Brad Edie's and killed him? What if it really was Virginia behind the wheel of that car? What if Walter woke up too soon? She comes home, pistol in hand. When he hears about Brad's death, Walter knows the truth, but he loves his wife. He can't turn her in, not when she denies everything. Yet, from that point on, he knows he's a marked man. Would a woman like that hesitate to consolidate her position by doing to Walter what she did to Brad? He might have taken to sleeping in a separate room, door locked, and his pistol under his pillow."

"You have a point," Hope admitted. "We don't know if Walter knew about his wife and Brad. I don't think he acted like he knew."

"Oh, you know how Mrs. Zalar said she never drove the route she took the night Edie died? She did drive it ... several times. We searched the camera footage and found her car."

"I see. I guess I should have expected that."

The detective said, "It will come up if she takes the stand. Once a liar, always a liar."

The house had been left a mess. The emergency personnel had tossed debris about, and the subsequent search had not been neatly performed. Hope didn't want to search. The police had been thorough. She wouldn't find anything of interest. Instead, she went to the bedroom. That was where she found the photo of Walter.

It was an 8x10, a good image and not too old. Hope snapped several pics of the photo, while the detective watched.

"You know that your chances of someone remembering him are next to zero," Detective Robinson said.

"I'm not overly optimistic," Hope answered.

"You could skip the drive and just tell her you couldn't find any leads."

"That would be cheating and lying. I'd rather waste the gas."

"Fair enough. I wish you luck."

"That's something, considering I might find something that ruins your case."

The detective nodded. "I'll take my chances."

Hope made a tour of the house before she left. She didn't discover anything that shed any light on

Virginia's predicament. Shaking her head, she left and drove home.

"When are you going to talk to Norrie?" Cori asked over a dinner of beef stew and salad.

"I have put it off, haven't I?" Hope answered. "I'll do it after dinner. You do know that I'm not at all sold on this manager stuff."

"I know. It scares me, too."

"Maybe we can work out something that makes sense."

"That would be great, Mom."

After dinner, Hope went up to her office where Max sat staring at the computer screen.

"Did you know that there are computer programs that translate from one language to another?" Max asked.

"I'm aware," Hope answered, "but I don't think they're perfect translators, if you know what I mean. Are you translating something?"

Max was dressed in a karate costume, complete with a black belt. He was hardly Asian, but he did look like a warrior.

"Korean to English, and I must say it is not going well. While the program spits out English, it is hardly passable, let alone publishable."

"So, a lot of rewriting?"

"First, I have to figure out the story. Some of this reads like what an elementary student would create."

"That must make it more than a little difficult."

"It's time for a break. I suspect you'd like some privacy?"

"I would, if you don't mind. I need to make a call I'd rather not make."

"The hardest kind. Good luck, Mrs. Herring."

Max disappeared, and Hope sat at her desk, pulling out her phone. Norrie answered on the second ring.

"Hello, Hope. Cori told me to expect a call."

"She's good that way, Norrie. It's about the manager situation."

"I know, and I apologize if I caused any consternation in your house. I simply thought that in today's world, singers start younger and younger."

"No one wants to fall behind. I know that. I also know that managers have to be aggressive. They have to work hard to place talent. Yet, I want Cori to have what I would call a normal life. I don't want her to feel isolated and committed to a schedule that robs her of her friendships, and she has schoolwork to keep up with, too."

"I understand. Managers come in many different

flavors. I think I might know one or two that would not press too hard. We all know stories of young performers who suffer from burnout or get into trouble with alcohol or drugs. No one wants that for Cori or for anyone. I'm on your side, Hope. I want what's best for Cori."

"I believe you. What's the next step?"

"With your permission, I'd like to introduce Cori to several managers who may not be the most high-powered in the business, but do their best to keep their clients sane and satisfied. Cori doesn't need Las Vegas yet."

"All right, go ahead and contact the ones you think will fit Cori and her protective mother."

"There's nothing wrong with being protective, Hope."

"I try to do my best. You'll call me before you introduce Cori to anyone?"

"Of course, she's a minor. I'll send along all the information I have also. I'm not going to hide anything from you. After all, the Internet has access to almost everything."

"We're on the same page."

After the call, Hope visited her daughter's room where Cori was listening to a podcast that Norrie had recommended. When she spotted her mother, she hit pause.

"Here's the deal," Hope said. "Norrie is going to contact some managers who she thinks will do the best for you. She will run them by me before she tells you. You might not think that's fair, but you're still a minor."

"And, you're still going to protect me, right?"

"I'll do my best, Cori. At the same time, I have to give you a chance to breathe. Flowers don't grow under a blanket."

"I understand. Thanks."

"In the meantime, you'll still take lessons from her. You'll still practice. You'll still do your homework and hang out with your friends. This is not a job or a career yet."

"Roger that."

"I'm driving to Chapel Hill after baking on Saturday. Want to come along?"

"Sure. UNC?"

"No, no fraternities this time. I'm trying to find out what Walter Zalar was doing there five months ago."

"Five months ago? Do you really think someone will remember him?"

"No, I don't think anyone will, but I promised

Mrs. Zalar that I would do it, so I will. I don't make promises unless I'm prepared to make good on them."

"Yeah, I know. Kids in school make promises all the time that don't mean anything. They just don't want to say no to anything."

"They'll grow out of that ... I hope. All right, get some sleep."

"Mom, if Norrie comes up with someone that we both like, does that mean I have to start really ... performing?"

"You don't have to do anything you don't want to do. However, a manager will work to place you, and once you sign a contract, you have to honor it. It's work, Cori, real work. You can't skip because you don't feel like doing it. You owe your manager and the person paying you. Think about that before you agree to anything."

Cori nodded.

∽

Hope considered Cori's hesitation even as she finished her Saturday morning bake session at the Butter Up bakery. Edsel, the owner, stopped Hope before she could slip out the door.

"Something bothering you?" Edsel asked.

"No, no, just the problems of an ordinary life that might become something other than ordinary."

"Need any help or advice?"

"Not at the moment, but if I find myself in too deep, can I call you?"

"Sugar, you can ask me for anything. You've helped me a lot more than I've helped you."

"Wish me luck."

"You don't need luck. You've got the goods. I have complete faith in you."

"Lend me some of your faith?"

Edsel laughed.

Cori was quiet on the drive to Chapel Hill. Hope noticed, but she didn't question. The teen was allowed to be something other than bubbly all the time. She was maturing. She might have real jobs soon. She might have pressures. That was something to consider. Not everyone responded well to pressure.

"Where are we going?" Cori asked.

"The Carolina Inn."

19

Hope and Cori spent an hour at the Carolina Inn, asking questions and showing the picture of Walter to anyone who would agree to look. As predicted, no one recognized the man. No one could explain what he had been doing in Chapel Hill. They had run into a dead end. As a last effort, Hope asked where someone staying at the Inn might go for breakfast or lunch. There was an answer to that question.

Frank's wasn't a typical diner. No vinyl, no chrome, no long counter. It featured lines of small tables all equipped with WI-FI connections and ports for recharging the devices that students carried everywhere. Even though it was a Saturday, many of the tables were occupied by students intently working on their laptops. Hope knew that modern education used computer-driven instruction. Students were obligated to check out class postings online. She and Cori found a small table, where Cori plugged in her phone. Hope laid out the pic of Walter.

"If I get a manager," Cori mused, "does that mean I have to share my money?"

"Managers don't work for free. Generally, though, they work on commission. That means their fee comes from what you're paid. If they can't place you in a paying job, they don't make money. That means they work hard."

"I don't think I'd like to work on commission."

"Salespeople often work on commission. When they're selling, they make good money. If they can't make a sale, well, that means hard times."

The waiter looked like a student—longish hair, jeans, tee, and sneakers. His beard was fashionably short; his glasses small and square. Hope wondered how he could see through them. She pointed to the pic.

"Have you ever seen this man?"

The waiter shook his head. "We have a lot of people come and go."

"I suspected as much. He stayed in the Carolina Inn some months ago. It's a long shot. If you could take the pic and show it to the other staff it would be very helpful."

"Sure, sure, someone might recognize him."

The waiter took the photo and walked off.

"That won't work," Cori said.

"I know," Hope answered. "Even if he does show it to the others, no one will recognize Walter."

"Why not?"

"Because they're mostly students, and students generally care about two things ... themselves and other students. I doubt anyone would notice an older man like Walter."

"You might be surprised."

"Right."

Hope and Cori were waiting for their orders to arrive when the door opened and a woman entered and stopped. She wore a green scarf over a bald head. No eyebrows, pale, and thin, Hope could tell the woman had experienced chemotherapy. She had survived, and that was a wonderful thing. Hope was surprised by what happened next. The woman held up a red rose and a silver coin.

Everyone in the restaurant began to clap. Hope was amazed. Those dedicated students stood and clapped. They were joined by all the waitstaff, men and women. The chefs and cooks emerged from the kitchen, and with them came the busboys and dishwashers. They all applauded the woman. They celebrated her victory.

"What's this all about?" Cori asked their waiter.

"She graduated chemo, and she's clean, no cancer anywhere," he answered.

"I got that," Cori said, "but how do you know?"

"The UNC cancer center is nearby. Lots of patients come here before or after an appointment. Rachel has been here many times before. So, whenever someone whips cancer, we applaud." He handed the pic to Hope. "Sorry, no one remembers him."

"It was a long shot," Hope said. "Thanks for asking."

Hope watched as two waitresses escorted Rachel to a table in the middle of the room. The clapping stopped only when Rachel sat, along with a man that had to be her husband. Hope could see tears on Rachel's cheeks, even as her husband grabbed her hands. It was a stirring moment.

"That's really cool," Cori said.

Hope nodded.

Cori added, "There's not much happiness for the ones who don't make it."

Hope sighed. "Not all news is good news."

Taking Chances

They were halfway back to Castle Park when Cori's phone chimed.

"It's Norrie," Cori said before she answered.

From the half conversation Hope could hear, it was obvious that Cori was talking to Norrie about a manager or managers. Half a conversation provided Hope with some information, but she felt she needed to know more of the details. Luckily, she also knew she wouldn't have to ask.

Cori soon ended the call.

"What did Norrie have to say?"

"She said she has a manager she wants me to meet. It's a woman Norrie has known for years. Junie is not the most popular or most successful manager in the music business, but Norrie says she's honest and a very hard worker. Junie has listened to my recordings, and she thinks I have talent and potential. So, the gigs she'll get for me are going to be small and cheap. No pressure. I have to do my best, nothing more. Norrie's going to call you about it."

"When do we meet Junie?"

"Two weeks, according to Norrie. In Wilmington. Junie is coming down for a visit. Like I said, she and Norrie are great friends."

"Right. Good. I would hate to have to fly somewhere. So, tell me, are you excited?"

"Yeah, I am. I mean, I'm scared too."

"You're supposed to be scared. Any time a person steps out of their bubble, they're scared. I remember the first time I taught a class without a real teacher in the room. I was certain the kids were going to laugh, disobey, and pretty much make my life a living hell. That didn't happen. I faked being confident. They bought it. Well, they didn't act up too much. Within a month, it was old hat. When you do what you fear, you soon lose the fear."

"Teachable moment?"

"Roger that."

Cori laughed. "I liked the applause."

"What?"

"In the restaurant. I liked it when they clapped for that woman."

"I liked it, too."

"Can I tell Lottie about the manager?"

"Do you want to?"

"Yes and no. I mean, it's not like I already have a manager. It's all just talk right now."

"But, you still want to share it, right?"

"People like to share good news."

Hope agreed, "Yep, it's the bad news that they hide."

"I'll call her."

"Good idea."

At home, Max was waiting for Hope. He was dressed in an old-time NY Yankee's uniform.

"Babe Ruth," Max said. "He was the greatest Yankee of all time, wasn't he?"

"Some people think so. He's one of the most famous. Why are you dressed like Babe?"

"Well, I was reading a blurb about him, and I discovered that in one game, he called his own homerun. He pointed to the bleachers and then hit the ball there. Isn't that fabulous?"

"It is indeed, if it's true. Many stories about famous people are more lore than fact."

"I'm going to believe it because I'm going to call my own homerun. I have a romance novel to edit. I'm going to say right now that I will finish it in forty-eight hours. Isn't that some sort of accomplishment?"

"Editing a novel in forty-eight hours is indeed a homerun, Max. When will you start?"

"I intend to commence as soon as I've finished chatting with you. I shall track my time on the computer clock to ensure that it will be accurate."

"We wouldn't want your record to be questioned."

"I sense a bit of mockery in your voice, but I shall

ignore it. I've come to the conclusion that I must devise my own challenges and meet them. You might blame yourself for that."

"Me? What did I do?"

"You solved the mystery of my murder. You removed the reason for my staying in this house. Ergo, you forced me to find other reasons."

"Guilty. I accept my fate." Hope laughed.

"I'm glad to find you in such a good mood. You must have solved your own mystery."

"I believe I have exhausted all explanations that might have helped Walter's wife. That makes her the killer. That might not be the outcome I wanted, but it seems inescapable."

"I'm not sorry for her if she did the deed. Justice demands that she pay for her nefarious ways."

"You're right, Max."

"Then, I am off on my record-breaking edit. Well, it's only my own record, but I will treat it like some worldwide record."

"As we all will."

"By the way, Mrs. Herring, I believe your latest artwork is hanging upside down."

Hope frowned. "What makes you say that?"

"The artist's signature is generally in the lower, lefthand corner, not the upper right."

"I know, but if I reverse it, the signature will be upside down."

"True, but you might try it." With a smile, Max disappeared.

Hope was about to discount his comment about the painting, when she thought she might flip it and see what it produced. After all, Walter had been known for painting art that changed based on one's perspective. Did the canvas produce a different effect if it was stood on its head?

"Tomorrow," Hope whispered to herself. "I'll do it tomorrow."

She poured herself a glass of wine and headed for the family room. After baking cakes and driving to Chapel Hill, she was tired. She needed some quiet minutes. Even as she sat, with Bijou pressed against her leg, she noticed the painting, prominently displayed according to Walter's instructions. Max's comment nagged at her. Clearly, she had hung the painting exactly right. Despite the signature in the upper right, the painting made sense. Max was simply mocking her for her mocking him.

But, what if....

Hope didn't want to admit that Max was right. If she didn't turn the canvas, she would be bitten by his observation over and over—every time she looked at the wall.

Bijou sat up, looked at the painting on the wall, and grumbled low in her throat.

"Okay, kitty." With a sigh, she pushed herself out of the comfortable chair and took the painting off the wall. She flipped it and leaned it against the wall, then, she stepped back. The painting was quite different from the new angle, and it was still fascinating. Yet, did it make more sense now? She couldn't tell. She supposed she had to put it back on the wall to make sure. With a sigh, she rehung the work, the signature now upside down. She wondered what kind of game Walter might have been playing, daring the owner to hang the painting in a traditional fashion. She took one step back.

Bijou trilled.

"I see it," a voice from the hall said.

Hope looked over her shoulder. Cori stood in the doorway. "See what?"

"The message."

"What message?"

"Come over here."

When Hope joined Cori, the different perspective did indeed produce words.

"What does it mean?" Cori asked.

"Tell me what you see."

"It says 'I DID IT.' What does that mean?"

"Step over there." Hope pointed, and Cori moved from the hallway to the other side of the room. "Still see it?"

"Yep. Why would he paint something like that?"

"Because he was a clever, vindictive man."

"Vindictive?"

"People get that way when they think they've been wronged."

"Who wronged him?"

"His wife mostly, I think." Hope headed for her phone. "Don't touch the painting. I need to talk to Detective Robinson."

20

Detective Robinson was waiting outside the house when Hope and Cori arrived. Hope found it difficult to read the detective's face. Was he happy to be there, or was he a bit miffed because it was a Sunday afternoon? She hoped he would give her a good listen.

"You said this is important," the detective began. "I hope so. I'm missing my nap."

"I want to thank you for meeting me," Hope said. "I don't know how important this will be. First question, did you talk to the person who did the autopsy?"

"I did. The autopsy, as you guessed, was limited. After all, the cause of death was easy ... poison. The tox screen proved that. There was no need to go any deeper."

"Exactly. But, he's going to go back and look, right?"

"I told him to, but he didn't like it."

"It can't be helped. You asked Virginia about a wig?"

"I did. She said she doesn't own a blond wig, as she is a blonde. However, she does own a red wig and a black wig. They're in her closet."

"You believe her?"

"I don't know why she would lie about a wig."

"Exactly. Shall we?"

"The sooner we get this over with the better."

The house was exactly as Hope remembered it—crime scene tape and fingerprint powder. The detective led the way to the primary bedroom and Virginia's closet. He stepped aside with a smile.

"Help yourself."

Hope stepped into the closet and turned on the light. It took less than five minutes to determine that there was no blond wig.

"Satisfied?" the detective asked as Hope stepped out of the closet.

"Yes and no. I need to keep looking."

Hope moved from Virginia's closet to Walter's. She turned on the light and stepped inside. She riffled through the clothes. It took four minutes to find the shoebox that held a blond wig.

"His closet?"

"Could you do a DNA test on it?" Hope asked.

"What do you think we'll find?"

"I think you'll find his DNA, not hers, and it's a woman's wig."

"Are you suggesting that Walter was some kind of crossdresser?"

"No, I don't think so. I think this is the wig he wore when he killed Brad Edie."

"One wig with his DNA won't prove that."

"No, but it's a start."

"Fair enough. What else?"

"His studio."

The attic was warm, but not hot. Air conditioning was needed by a painter. Walter's canvases were spread all about. Some had been stacked, others leaned against the walls, and several were hanging from the rafters.

"What are we looking for?" Detective Robinson asked.

"You're aware of his style?" Hope asked.

"Yeah, the paintings become optical illusions the longer you look at them."

"Exactly. I think Walter created some that will

tell us more about the death of Brad Edie and Walter's own death."

"There are a lot of paintings in here."

"I think we need to concentrate on the newest ones. They're all dated, aren't they?"

"I sure hope so."

"Cori, help us look for paintings finished in the last year or any painting that doesn't have a date."

"Roger that," Cori replied.

The next thirty minutes were filled with the three sifting through the stacks of paintings, separating the most recent from older efforts. Hope was sweating as they finished. She looked at half a dozen paintings lined up against one wall.

"All right," Detective Robinson said. "What now?"

"Obviously, Walter didn't paint the murder scene in a way we would recognize so, I'm going to slowly rotate the paintings. You two see if there is something hidden in the colors."

"I should do that," Cori said.

"No, I want your young eyes to take a look. I might be biased to see something that isn't really there."

Hope worked slowly through the first three paintings. Nothing. While the images did change, they didn't provide any connection to either death. The fourth painting was different. She had to turn it on its head to make the detective whistle.

"What the...?" he said. "It's her, and she's shooting him."

"That's really cool," Cori added.

Hope stepped away from the painting and joined the others. The painting did indeed show a blond woman who looked remarkably like Virginia firing a pistol at Brad Edie.

"How did he do that?" Cori asked.

"He worked long and hard on it."

"But, it doesn't prove that Walter was Virginia in disguise."

"I agree, but it raises more doubt."

Hope walked back to the wall and flipped the next painting. It showed Walter on his phone, standing over a sleeping Virginia.

"The murder phone call," Hope said when she saw the painting. "She's sleeping. He's dying. I don't think he could have painted this if he hadn't been planning it."

"She might have painted it," the detective offered.

"No, I don't think she has a clue as to how to create something like this. It was all Walter."

"We can't really prove that. Why would Walter paint these scenes?"

"Here is what I think," Hope began. "Walter knew about his wife and Brad Edie. No one thinks Walter is the kind of man who would murder someone. I believe he loved his wife, but she had betrayed him. He might have coped with the knowledge and allowed the affair to run out, which it did."

"Then, why would he kill?" Cori asked.

"Because he was dying," Hope answered. "Virginia told me he had cancer."

"But he told you there was nothing wrong with him," Detective Robinson said.

"He knew he was sick, but he didn't want others to know. He went to Chapel Hill and the university health providers to see what could be done. I'm guessing the prognosis was terminal. That made him desperate to see justice done. He drugged his wife, put on the blond wig, and drove to Brad's house. He shot Brad with her pistol and drove home."

"The poisoning?"

"A dying man might want to get back at the person who wronged him. Walter drugged his wife and took the poison. Then, when he knew he couldn't be saved or questioned, he called for help.

He made sure to tell the dispatcher that his wife had poisoned him."

"A death bed confession?"

"Well, he didn't confess."

"I don't get it. If he wanted to get back at her, why not poison her?"

Hope explained, "I think he wanted her to suffer. Spending years in prison for something she hadn't done would be a good punishment."

"That's loony," Cori said.

"Why the paintings though?" Detective Robinson asked. "He could have made sure she went to prison even if he hadn't painted them."

"I think Walter was pretty sure no one would ever suspect that he had some untreatable condition. I mean, if they found it in an autopsy, they would think it hadn't been discovered. After all, he hadn't used any local doctors. These paintings were done before the deaths. No one would be looking for the hidden message. I'm guessing it would take years to find the messages, if ever."

"More work, right?" Detective Robinson said.

Hope nodded. "Since he's dead, I think you might be able to find the doctor in Chapel Hill who examined Walter. Go back some months in his credit card records, and you might find a payment. Walter didn't think you would investigate him since he was the victim."

"Help me take these out to the car?" the detective asked. "They're evidence now."

"You know," Cori said as she grabbed a canvas, "this makes me wonder about what sort of messages are hidden in old paintings. What do you think, some hidden treasure?"

"I'm sure you can find instructions to the fountain of youth and Shangri-la," Hope told her.

Cori laughed. "Why would I need the fountain of youth?"

"Because sooner or later, you'll get old."

"Hah! Not a chance."

21

"I'm leaving Castle Park."

Hope looked across the table where Virginia played with her coffee cup.

"You don't have to," Hope said.

"I know, but I think it's for the best. Even though I had nothing to do with the deaths of Brad and Walter, a lot of people won't believe it, not really. There will always be some doubt, you know?"

"I do. People don't forget easily, especially people who have to deal with their own guilt."

"Yes, there's that."

"You sold the house already?"

Virginia shook her head. She had lost some weight while in jail. There was no luster in her hair or in her eyes.

"No, the house is still for sale. Know anyone who might want it?"

"I'll keep my eyes and ears open," Hope told her.

"Thanks, and I know I've said this before, but thank you for solving the mystery." Her nervous fingers danced around the cup. "If you had asked me a year ago if I thought Walter was capable of jealousy and murder, I would have laughed. I mean, he was never the alpha male, if you know what I mean."

"I won't speculate on the pain he must have felt," Hope said.

"I know, I know. His wife was unfaithful, and he had untreatable cancer. That's a lot to bear. I like ... I like to think that the cancer warped his thinking. He wouldn't have done what he did if he'd been well."

"Probably not."

Virginia looked off across the room for a few seconds. "I know he wanted to send me to prison for a long time. That stings. I mean, we were married. Maybe we could have talked it out. I suppose he was just getting even for the affair I didn't tell him about."

"I've found, Virginia, that you can't go back, and you shouldn't second guess. What has passed has passed."

"I should have paid more attention to his feelings."

"We all wear blinders at times."

Cori appeared in the doorway. "Hello, Mrs. Zalar."

"Hello, Cori. You look all dressed up."

"I have an appointment with my voice coach."

"You're a great singer. How goes it?"

"I'm not so great, but I am progressing. That's a good thing."

Virginia stood. "Well, then, I need to be off."

Hope walked Virginia to the front door, where they hugged. She felt Virginia shudder.

"You're the heroine," Virginia said. "If you ever need anything, anything at all, call me. I'll help."

"Someday, I just might take you up on that."

Virginia chuckled and walked out. Hope watched until the car had driven off.

"It's time," Cori said.

Hope turned and regarded a daughter that looked older than she was.

"Time to meet the manager?" Hope asked.

"Possible manager," Cori said. "She has to like me as much as she likes my voice."

"Piece of cake," Max said.

Hope turned to face Max, who smiled.

"Thanks, Max," Cori told the ghost.

"Hold down the fort," Hope told him.

"I shall endeavor to do so. All will be well when you return."

Hope wrapped an arm around Cori's shoulders. "Let's go. You'll knock 'em dead."

Bijou trilled with happiness as she watched mother and daughter leave the house together.

THANK YOU FOR READING!

Books by J.A. Whiting can be found here:
amazon.com/author/jawhiting

To hear about new books and book sales, please sign up for our mailing list at:
jawhiting.com

Your email will never be sold, shared, or spammed.

If you enjoyed the book, please consider leaving a review. A few words are all that's needed. It would be very much appreciated.

BOOKS BY J.A. WHITING & NELL MCCARTHY

HOPE HERRING PARANORMAL COZY MYSTERIES

TIPPERARY CARRIAGE COMPANY COZY MYSTERIES

BOOKS BY J. A. WHITING

SWEET COVE PARANORMAL COZY MYSTERIES

LIN COFFIN PARANORMAL COZY MYSTERIES

CLAIRE ROLLINS PARANORMAL COZY MYSTERIES

MURDER POSSE PARANORMAL COZY MYSTERIES

PAXTON PARK PARANORMAL COZY MYSTERIES

ELLA DANIELS WITCH COZY MYSTERIES

SEEING COLORS PARANORMAL COZY MYSTERIES

OLIVIA MILLER MYSTERIES (not cozy)

SWEET ROMANCES by JENA WINTER

COZY BOX SETS

BOOKS BY J.A. WHITING & ARIEL SLICK

GOOD HARBOR WITCHES PARANORMAL COZY MYSTERIES

BOOKS BY J.A. WHITING & AMANDA DIAMOND

PEACHTREE POINT COZY MYSTERIES

DIGGING UP SECRETS PARANORMAL COZY MYSTERIES

BOOKS BY J.A. WHITING & MAY STENMARK

MAGICAL SLEUTH PARANORMAL WOMEN'S FICTION COZY MYSTERIES

HALF MOON PARANORMAL MYSTERIES

VISIT US

jawhiting.com

bookbub.com/authors/j-a-whiting

amazon.com/author/jawhiting

facebook.com/jawhitingauthor

bingebooks.com/author/ja-whiting

J A WHITING
Books and More

Printed in Great Britain
by Amazon